# Sage of Darkness

Jose A. Sanchez

ISBN: 9798841949299

# CONTENTS

# ACKNOWLEDGMENTS

Thank you, Brittany, Arian, Grace, Marirosa, and all of the writers on Instagram that I reached out to. Your input and advice helped an idea become a reality.

# Prologue

## "The Worst Enemy"

This was the end of a long Journey. A journey full of blood, sweat, tears, immeasurable stress, and effort. Miles upon miles of hiking through mountains with obstacles everywhere in between. Deep canyons and splintered rock that cut deep into the skin. High altitudes, thin air that made it difficult to breathe. She had made her way through hundreds of winding roads, cliffs that overlooked the ocean, passed through empty cities, and empty schools. She had bloody sweat that got into her eyes, and reluctant tears that she was ashamed to let out. Tears that she had been holding back for years. After the mental anguish of reaching for something that you've been working for, years of effort. Nothing to drive forward other than the promise of what lies at the end, and the hope that that promise is true.

"A rising sun waits for you at the end of this path, along with a shadow that will guide you." That's what she was told. By a voice she didn't know, but somehow recognized. An answer to the questions she had been asking since her adolescence. A solution to a problem. A problem she couldn't define. A problem that she wasn't even sure existed. A way to prove herself worthy to no one in particular. To prove herself to everyone that mattered. To win a battle that was not defined by any physical constraints.

**So close. So close but so far. It's never enough. She tried getting up.**

"One!" The crowd is screaming, chanting, going wild and echoes yells all throughout the air and she tries to recover off the canvas.

"Two!" She is still in a haze. A small thought lingering in her head saying she should just give it up.

"Three!"

"Get up!", she thought to herself. "I can't now! Not after everything I've worked for!"

"Four!" "Five!" "Six!" She tried getting up, but her body isn't responding. Crumbling at every effort to stand.

"Seven!" I've been through so much worse than this, goddamn it! Why won't my body move?!"

"Eight! Nine!"

"For god's sake, get up!! Get! Up!" With one glove on her knee and one on the ground, she slowly started to rise.

"I can do this!! I can do this!! I WON'T stop!!" She thought as she got up to her feet and put her gloves back up.

Anxiety.

The bell rang as she collapsed again. Her entire body giving out, only one thought ran through her mind.

"I'm so fucking worthless."

She found a cave at the top of the peak that she finally reached. A cave that descended down deep into the mountains. Inside smelled of fresh water and salted rock. A surprisingly pleasant aroma. But as she took steps closer to it, she felt a dark presence. A powerful hatred lurking inside. The cave was damn near pitch black, and she could barely see a pathway to walk in.

She winced and held her hands to her chest.

A voice in her mind asked if she was really willing to go inside. Go inside such a frightening darkness and seek what she wanted? Is she really ok with going inside and possibly never coming out?

She took a deep breath, clenched her fists, and put them to her sides and answered the voice.

"Yes."

She took those oh-so-very-important steps to enter the cave that smelt so natural and pleasant but felt so very wrong to enter. As she walked, she put her hands against the walls of the cave to guide her. The rough cave walls had a light, cool moisture to them. She was barely able to see what was in front of her and this action was necessary to keep stable as she walked further in. She caught a few glimpses of what seemed to be scrolls with paintings on them.

She continued on deeper and deeper until she found herself in a large, dimly lit room. She glanced side to side and realized that it was a shrine. The shrine that she was told about. It seemed to be rustic for someone she was told was so wise. Essentially a cave with some minor man-made moderations to it. One single candle in the middle to give light to the surroundings. She noticed some more scrolls with black painted sketches on the walls with unlit candles beneath each. Some scrolls seemed to have an image of buildings, others of some type of vegetations, and others of spiderwebs, and a waterfall? They were difficult to look at with such little light.

After looking around for a couple of minutes to admire the simplistic beauty of the entire shrine she took a few more steps forward and found some steps that went up. She walked up the crudely built steps until she came face to face with someone.

The Sage she had heard about was sitting on a rounded stalagmite with a thin mat on top of it in the back of the small shrine. The Sage was nothing like what she thought any type of wise man would be like. A very large man, shaped like a man who carried boulders for fun. He wore a black hoodie, with jeans, and black combat boots. His attire covered his entire body, showing no skin. A mask covering his face had an evil grin on it.

She could feel the aura of his presence. He seemed angry, yet peaceful. Full of hatred and he knew what he was filled with and accepted it. A peaceful kind of chaos inside. And yet he projected all this while wearing that daunting mask.

Looking around, the girl noticed more scrolls of what seemed to be the same paintings. But these scrolls barely had anything on them. They seemed to be the beginning of rough drafts of landscape paintings. All with another unlit candle under them.

She wondered why he was called the sage of darkness. If darkness was supposed to be where the wicked lurks, how can one be a sage of it? How can something of malcontent be wise in any way? How can someone be so clearly full of hatred and anger yet peaceful like this sage was?

**This time would be different. She refused to lose again. She started training twice as hard and trained her mind ever more so. Her shame gave her fuel, her anger was a fire that drove her forward. Her pent-up hatred grew. It was almost as if these emotions were taking the form of a weapon that she was able to use. A terrible weapon.**

The Sage stared at her, as if he already knew what she was going to say. An intense yet calm, mask worn stare that looked into her soul.

"Master..." She said with the utmost conviction. "I wanna overcome."

The Sage waited for her to continue talking, his posture and aura giving the impression that he already knew what she was going to say before she said it.

He glared at her with the same intense, yet calm stare. "And just what is it you wish to overcome?" A stern voice that echoed through the shrine.

**The bell rang. The crowd cheered at the upset for her winning in a 1 to 50 chance. She saw her opponent crying and her trainers consoling her. For some reason, despite her past humiliation at the hands of the very same opponent, she couldn't help but feel sorry for her opponent. This made her wonder who her anger and hatred were directed towards in the first place. If she wasn't trying to defeat her opponent, who was she fighting against?**

Her thoughts raced. Flashbacks to everything she had been through. All she has faced in her life. Being born into a family that didn't want her, cast her aside and being forced in a home with a hateful set of controlling dogmatic parents that would beat her. Studying and scratching her way into a chance at a good education. Pushing her body to the absolute limit of what she thought she could do though her training, then pushing herself even further. All her depressive episodes and suicidal thoughts. She thought of the many arduous trials that she climbed to get to this very place. All of her battles, physical and mental. The very path through the winding mountain trails, thorns, poison, lakes, and wild animals she went through to come to see the Sage face to face. She had already overcome all these things by herself, what was left?

She looked down and stuttered as she tried to form a cohesive sentence. After her flashbacks, her utmost conviction turned into confusion and a loss for words.

"I... I don't know." She said.

**Not many know what it is like to be born into a family that doesn't want you. And even fewer know what it's like to be born with abusive foster parents. Filled with drugs and gunshots all around the neighborhood. How many also know what it is to have her young innocence corrupted by the hands of wrinkled old men and bigger classmates. To have her intellect stifled by words of discouragement from the mouth of the old nuns and priests. The ones who were supposed to protect and guide her. Yet for all this, how many know the courage it takes to run and leave the forsaken place that one might have been forced into? She rose above her fears of the unknown to get to a better place. Yet the shame of her origins and past**

**would haunt her for the rest of her life. A weight she would carry with a strong face and a stronger will.**

The Sage let out a light chuckle as if her answer was proving a prediction. "You have a strong look in your eye. An un-shatterable will. A heart that shines with passion. Your strength a bright light that illuminates your entire soul.  Yet, for all your strength, you are so easily defeated by your worst enemy."

She didn't understand, but she had faith in the undeniable wisdom of one called a Sage.

"Who is my worst enemy, master? What is it that I need to overcome? If I have already overcome all these trials and obstacles, what else is left? Please tell me, I'll do anything I need to!"

The sage got up off his sitting mat that was on top of that flat stalagmite and started walking towards her until he was an arms distance away and stopped. He stood motionless until reaching out his hand to place it on her shoulder.

**Days upon days studying. Obtaining a basic understanding of everything that exists, how to speak with elegance, the world of numbers. Advanced placement tests to get into a college that no one expected her to qualify for. How sad she must have felt, to let her anxiety get the better of her. Math and physics. How a black hole is everything in a point of nothing. How dividing something by nothing is not possible because it means infinity. Everything. To let something as petulant as nerves keep her from grabbing a hold of something she had been working so hard for.**

"I know you will do whatever you need to. But what if you need to do nothing? What if you need to do everything? How will you possibly fight against fighting against everything that matters? How will you cope with swinging you fists at the air and meditating on oblivion? How will you learn of nothing?"

She raised her eyebrow and puckered her lips to give an expression of 'what the actual fuck'. She had no idea what he was talking about.

The Sage let out another small chuckle, turned, and started to walk towards the back of the shrine.

"Come, lass. You worst enemy is waiting."

**This was her last chance. The placement tests. She knew that advanced placement exams for much more difficult than SATs. This score could be her retribution for her recent perceived failures. She learned how to deal with her anxieties. And she refused to let this opportunity slip by. Her efforts rewarded, yet oddly unsatisfying. How could she not feel happy after reaching a goal that she was unable to achieve before?**

The Sage led her into an entrance of another deeper cave. The farther they went in the darker it got and the thinner the air became. They reached a dead end. Nothing there but a large room laced with granite and black stone.

The Sage pulled matches from his pocket and lit a candle that was in the middle of the room. After light from the candle made everything in the room visible, She searched around side to side, attempting to analyze the area. All the while wondering what the Sage brought her here for.

"Look to your front." Said the Sage.

**Contrary to popular belief, jumping off a building, pulling the trigger to a gun held at the temple of your head. These things are not for the cowardly. But they do not take courage, either. All it takes is a concluded mind. Many thoughts and feelings raced through her head as she contemplated jumping off the cliff into the pointed rocks below. The warm sunlight heating up her skin as the cool afternoon breeze flowed through her hair. For all her triumphs, for all her victories, she still felt defeated. As if her nameless and shapeless enemy won every battle she had lost and also won the battles that she had won. It made no sense. The only way she could atone for these lost victories was to end it all. Yet she stepped down. She would not see her nameless enemy win so easily.**

She quickly turned her head and saw a mirror hanging from a pitch-black wall of stone at a dead end. The Sage slowly and calmly walked forward until he stood right next to the mirror leaning against the black stone wall of the cave with his arms crossed.

He tilted his mask covered face towards the girl. "Stand in front of the mirror and look directly at your reflection."

The girl did as she was instructed and took a few steps and stood directly in front of the mirror. Her entire face remained expression-less as she gazed into the mirror. Her reflection slowly started to change into a black silhouette. The girl shifted her head back in confusion to what was happening. After her reflection finished shifting its appearance into a solid shadow that took the exact shape of the girl, it took a step forward and came out of the mirror.

There it stood, in all its feculent splendor in the candle lit dead end of the cave, right next to the Sage. The girl's hatred swelled up within her, causing her to tighten her fists and stiffen her entire body. Her anger filled her lungs causing her breaths to become rapid and powerful. Nostrils flaring, a loathing she never realized had been within her all this time.

The intense silence led to heavy breaths and a flurry of hellish heartbeats. All before a chaotic awakening from a conscience slumber.

**Therapy was always seen as a thing of weakness to most of the people she associated herself with. But despite that natural reluctance to admitting she needed help, she laid down her pride. Every session she went to had helped her understand herself more. She did not have demons. She WAS her demon. Yet therapy was not the solution to the inner angst she still felt after all these years. Her therapist told her that she did not need to prove her worth to others. She had even tried looking into the mirror and telling her reflection that she was worth it. She gazed into her reflection's eyes. Then analyzed her body and saw her reflection shake her head. The words of her therapist sounded like something she had been needing to hear, but it was not quite the answer she was looking for. Just a map to a place that might allow her to find the answer.**

The shadow-like creature that came out of the blackened mirror was the visible personification of all her anger. Her shame. Her hatred. Her faulty perceptions. Her depression. Her darkness. Like looking into a black mirror, a darkened reflection of who she thought she was, the thing she had been trying to destroy, the problem she had been facing, the person all her anger was directed towards. The very thing she had truly been fighting against. Throughout all her matches, her studies, her pride. The anxiety she fought against. She had not been trying to prove her worth to anyone but this voice in the back of her head that said she was worthless. Her own voice. Her worst enemy.

Herself.

She lunged forward and attacked the figure with an unparalleled ferocity. Yet every one of her blows added to the power of her worst enemy. The more her anger grew, the bigger the frown of her enemy. The more hatred in her screams, the more power her worst enemy had in its strikes. Every blow was countered by an even stronger blow, every attack stifled by her worst enemy. The young girls strikes' blocked perfectly by the shadow creature, yet every blow given hurt her limbs as she tried blocking. But for all the fighting, her enemy seemed to be defending more than anything.

She just couldn't figure it out. Was this creature the energy from her pent-up anger and hatred that she never let out? Was this the concept of energy not being able to be destroyed that she learned in school? If energy cannot be destroyed, was this where her pent-up emotions went to? Her mind raced as she fought harder and harder. But her enemy just grew and grew along with her anger. Small tears began to form in the corner of her eyes as she became more and more confused, not knowing what to do.

The Sage began to speak. A clear, audible, calm, and powerful voice. A soothing tone. A voice of acceptance and strength.

"How would you react when you need to do nothing? When doing nothing means everything? When you realize everyone that matters is no one? When you need to prove yourself to no one? Not even yourself?"

She stopped attacking her worst enemy to hear the words of the sage. And as she did, her worst enemy stopped as well.

The Sage began to speak again.

"You wondered how there can be a Sage of Darkness. How can hatred be wise? My dear, hatred is not the counterpart of love, but its sister. Anger is simply an emotion. And like me, it's the emotion you naturally drift towards. You've accepted your light and willpower as a burning fire that shines light all over your soul, yet you won't accept the shadows that are cast from that very light. Shadows that take the shape of who you are."

She stopped fighting and thought at what the Sage said. How would she react when what she needed to do was nothing, yet everything? The very act of doing nothing meant everything. To fight against everyone that matters?

She paused and looked at her worst enemy. Her enemy looking back as if waiting for her to say something. The body language of her worst enemy calling for a warm embrace.

Breathing heavily, she started to talk in spurts.

"So…" She panted.

"I don't need to prove myself to anyone…"

"… not even… myself?" Her words cut by heavy breaths.

As she attempted to gather her thoughts and calm herself, her worst enemy began shrinking in size. Her frown disappeared into what seemed to be a small smile.

Eventually, her worst enemy shrank to the same size as the young woman and mimicked her calmness.

And she realized that she did not need to fight her darkness to defeat it. She has been fighting so much all her life yet could not come to terms with herself. She did not need to prove her worth to anyone, not even herself.  She had stripped away the layers of her entire being until nothing but her bare soul was left. There was a beautiful light complimented with a chaotically beautiful darkness. And instead of fighting it, she would accept it. Not just the light of her love and passion, but the darkness of who she was.

Her body took a welcoming stance as she walked towards her worst enemy. And her worst enemy walked towards her as well. She reached out her hand. The figure reached its hand as well.

And it is then that she gained her greatest ally.

# <u>Authors note(s)</u>

Thank you for taking the time to read 'Sage of Darkness'. Your support is greatly appreciated, and I hope you enjoy reading the journey as much as I enjoyed writing it. There are some things you should know before moving forward.

- Most chapters are broken up into a "part 1" and a "part 2". The part 1s are the main character going through her usual life in reality. The part 2s are a dream sequence taking place as it relates to the story.
- Many names are references to famous philosophers, psychologists, or simply words in Latin or Japanese.
- Each dream is based on a poem located in the back of the book.
- Some chapters can be graphic and triggering.

Thank you again for reading, and I hope you enjoy the story.

# Chapter 1

# Part 1

The girl woke up to rays of light shining on her face through the curtains. The birds gently chirping outside and the sound of a garbage truck outside picking up bins. She got up and quickly walked to her mirror to verify who she was. For a split second she saw her shadow smiling in the mirror before it reflected her own face. Dark green eyes, shoulder length black hair spiked at the tips and sun kissed brown skin.

The dream was as vivid as real life. Her heavy breathing and blows she gave and took felt as real as all of her matches in real life. The desperation and anger, pulse racing and drops of blood dropping were all so vivid. The words that the Sage spoke still resonated with her.

She remembered what the Sage from her dreams had shown her. An unexpected lesson she never realized she needed. She has accepted all of herself and was ready to dive in deeper.

Excited to start her new life with her newfound perspective, she had almost forgot that today was her first day of college. It was time to get ready. As she fixed up her hair, she knew that the Sage would once again show the girl her innermost unconscious thoughts. Putting on her low-cut black t shirt she knew she would begin to analyze what she hated and loved, and for what reasons. She put on her denim jeans and calf high black combat boots and began to wonder what has really kept her going all this time.

From her bed area to the entrance of her studio apartment door. From the door to the parking lot entrance. From the parking lot entrance to her car. From her car to the streets, and from the streets to the campus. Every little detail of what she did was becoming relevant to her. She was becoming more aware of her actions now.

After 10 minutes of walking and looking around at her new environment, she finally reached her building number. Labeled 1111. The girl was usually early to events but wasn't accustomed to college life. Most of the class was already here. She got to her first class just in time and the professor walked in right behind her. A short, young clean-shaven man with slicked back brown hair. He set down his things and began the expected introductions.

"Hello class, my name is Professor Niels, and I will be instructing this introduction to chemistry class." He spoke with sheer experience and in the friendliest tone one can imagine. Calm, collected, but very audible. "Considering this is a small class, let's all go around and introduce ourselves and share something you'd like to share with everyone else."

Her curiosity was tugged as each student introduced themselves with personal facts. Mostly kids straight out of high school, some early 20-year-olds trying college out after a couple years of working with their parents, some veterans, and older people finally following their dreams of education. Some decided to read excerpts from great philosophers that they took from their previous year philosophy classes after they gave their names, thinking they might earn some intellectual points from the other students. Some read pieces from Shakespeare that they believed everyone should know. Some just shared facts about themselves. The veterans shared some experiences from being in the military, and some of the older students shared some life advice, primarily aimed at the younger students.

As the introductions came closer and closer to the girl, she noticed a young man a few seats down from where she was frantically writing something down, clearly trying to finish before it was his turn. He seemed to make it just in time.

The young man stood up, shook himself of any nerves he had, and spoke.

"Hey, everyone. My name is Eros, this is my 2nd year and I'm a physics major. But I also love writing poetry. And I decided to write something that related to this class."

Eros cleared his throat.

"This poem is called 'Atomic dismantling'

*Let's find out what makes you tick*
*We'll take you apart piece by piece*

*First let's dig into your memories*
*Repressed memories*
*Happy memories*
*Sad memories*

*Then let's take a look at your thoughts and emotions*
*The kind of thoughts you have when no one is looking*
*What do you think about when it's late at night and you can't sleep?*
*What do you feel when you're by yourself?*

*When kind of emotions do you have with your friends?*
*What do you feel when you think about yourself?*

*Let's begin looking at your weaknesses, strengths and*
*interests*
*The things that bring you down*
*The things that bring you up*
*Things that you do to keep yourself occupied*
*Objects or ideas that make you smile*

*Now let's look at your chemical makeup*
*Your levels of dopamine*
*Do you lack serotonin?*
*What triggers your adrenaline?*

*Now let's look into your heart*
*Things that you live for*
*Things that keep you going*
*The people you love*
*I sincerely hope that I am somewhere in there"*

As he finished, the young woman began lightly clapping her hands, admiring the poem subject matter and the courage of the young student to give a small performance as an introduction. The class followed and gave a light applause and Professor Niels congratulated the young man for writing something so relevant on the spot. And the introductions continued.

The girl's turn was getting closer and closer. As the student before the girl finished her introduction, Professor Niels looked at the girl and smiled.

"Young lady in the black shirt. Why don't you go ahead and introduce yourself and share something with the class?"

She stood up and began to lightly tremble. She wasn't used to speaking in front of large groups of people, but she stood up, swallowed hard, cleared her throat, and went for it.

"Hi, everyone. It's my first year here at Jannah university. I worked a year after secondary school to save up and I'm currently working part time." The girl shakily said.

"And your name?" Professor Niels asked with a warm smile.

"My… my name is Era.", she said with a mellifluous voice.

All eyes and ears still on her, waiting for her to finish.

"It's Uhm... It's short for Erebus." She said while giving an awkward grin.

After the introductions were done, the class slowly started clapping, student by student. And by the time the last one slapped their hands together; the class was over. The professor dismissed the class by giving some reading instructions for homework and all of the students got up and made their way towards their corresponding destinations. Era stayed behind until all the students were gone. She placed her elbow on the desk, leaned into her hand, and began to get lost in her thoughts. Soaking in everything that happened. With each student coming in, taking up seats, Era decided to get up and leave.

Era headed out of the class and walked from the exit of the classroom to the exit of the building, to one of the walkways of the campus. Headed to her next class, she noticed a couple of people eyeing her up, or others glancing at her with disgust. Her immediate thought was to break their nose for looking at her wrong. The social interactions and introductions of the students took a toll on her, and she was feeling irritable. But she managed to maintain her composure as the day went on.

The rest of her classes consisted of biology and the corresponding labs for chemistry and biology. The classes and labs were short, as the teachers and lab instructors simply handed out a syllabus and told everyone to read some chapters and look over the guidelines for the upcoming dissections of animals and chemistry experiments. The chance to learn excited Era.

After the day of her classes was done, Era decided to flex her new age and hit up a local bar. Her birthday had just passed a couple months ago, and she was finally able to legally drink. She made her way to a bar named 'The Elysium Pub', which had a lot of positive reviews.

After parking, she walked inside and headed towards the main counter. It was a nice set up. Plenty of space, places to sit, art covering the walls, and a little speaker off in the corner on top of a small stage. Probably for karaoke.

She sat down and waited for the bartender. He was facing the opposite direction of Era, facing the sink, cleaning some glasses that a previous customer had left. After finishing, he turned around and started walking towards her.

As he walked towards her, she recognized his face. It was the boy who read the poem in the chemistry class.

"What can I get you?" The bartender boy said with a huge, warm smile. He leaned in with his arms on the table, looking directly at Era.

"A screwdriver sounds good. Said Era. And the bartender boy happily obliged.

After some light chatter and drinking, Era decided to head home. She picked up her things and headed towards her car. As she started driving, she began wondering if she'd come across the Sage again in her dreams again.

She arrived home, ate her usual health-oriented food, showered, meditated on what she had learned that day, and laid down. After a long day it only took a couple of seconds of laying down for her eyes to shut. And she slowly drifted off into her own little world.

# Part 2

## "Atomic dismantling"

Era found herself standing in front of the Sage once again. The Sage stood there, tall and powerful despite wearing a hoodie that covered his entire upper body. He stood there silently, calm and relaxed. Waiting. Era opened her mouth in an attempt to speak, but before she could say anything, the Sage said, "That was a pretty interesting poem that kid read in the class, wasn't it Era? I really enjoyed it."

Era looked at the Sage confused, Squinting her eyes and puckering her lips, wondering how he knew about the poem.

"I really like the concept of what he was talking about." He said." Now come with me."

Era noticed they were no longer at the shrine where they met. They seemed to be in what look liked a laboratory. Full of beakers with chemicals and white boards with various chemical equations. As Era looked around, she wondered why the Sage would be in a laboratory instead of the previously seen shrine which seemed to be his home. They kept walking until they came to what looked to be an operating room. Now even more confused, Era began to wonder what lunacy the Sage must have been going through to go from a shrine to a laboratory, to an operating room. They walked to an operating table and the sage turned to her.

"Lay down, Era." The Sage calmly instructed.

As she climbed on and slowly laid down, the Sage began to pick up a scalpel. But Era held absolutely no fear. She didn't whine, wince, or even flinch. All she did was wonder what the Sage was thinking.

"That poem that young man read today. I've been pondering on it all day." Informed the Sage. "I thought we could both explore the theme of it together."

Era raised her eyebrow. Everything from the day unto now was connected. Then she realized what was about to happen. And it filled her with excitement.

"Now, Era. Let's take you apart piece by piece."

The Sage carefully dug the scalpel into her head. Blood dripped down to the crevices of her eyes, forming little pools until finally dropping down like tears. The Sage continued cutting until the top of her head was open and he pulled her brain out. After gently removing it, he started walking towards the counter.

"You can get up, Era. Come over here."

Era awkwardly got up, inner cranium showing. Then walked towards the counter.

The Sage placed the brain on what seemed to be a cutting board. He then took another scalpel and began cutting her brain up.

"You see, Era. Your brain holds your psyche. And if we can pick it apart, determine what is inside it and what made it form, we'll learn what makes you tick. Here in this part, you can see the traumas of what has happened to you in the past. This trauma can throw chemicals in your brain off and make you sad. Here, you can see this part of your brain light up when you in something you enjoy doing. Here are the memories from your childhood making you have a disdain for this activity and the memory of this song make you react with tears. And here I am, in the very back of your brain. The part that houses your unconscious."

The Sage continued, "Here are your serotonin receptors. You've been lacking it for years. Here are the dopamine receptors that kick into overdrive when you finally found the truth that you've been needing to hear."

Era looked intently at her brain. Wondering how much more she could pick it apart to see why she is the way she is.

The sage finished his explanation and then picked up her chopped-up brain and shoved it back into her head and slammed the top of her cranium back on. Hardly putting in any effort, he sewed Era's head back together to prevent her brains from spilling out. But it barely worked. With every movement a sloshing sound would echo faintly in he room and every time Era tilted her head or took a step some chunks of brain and blood would hit the ground beneath them.

"There, Era. Now lay back on the table, please."

Era heeded and wondered what would be next as she calmly walked back to the table. The Sage picked up another scalpel and slowly inserted it into her chest. Carefully slicing and dicing, he carved out her heart. After placing some stents to hold her chest cavity open, he pulled out her heart. He wasn't as careful as he was with her brain, essentially yanking it out. The arteries stretched and made sloshing noise and the sage took a pair of scissors and cut them all to separate the heart.

Holding it in one of his hands he began to walk towards the exit of the operating room. He waved Era over and they both started walking back towards the chemistry lab. Era began wondering what the chemistry lab could have to do with all this.

The Sage began separating various fluids from the heart into vials. Era looked at him as he crudely began using Bunsen burners to heat up her blood and other fluids. It made no sense.

"Here, Era. You can see the different elements of your blood react differently with the environment. This is your father's blood, and this is your mother's blood. And if we break it down further, we can separate them further into your grandparents' blood. Your bloodline gives you a predisposition to have an issue with addiction, or a tendency to be emotional. Some people have a genetic predisposition to diabetes or heart diseases. Some people even have a genetic predisposition to be happy or sad."

The sage then took her heart fluids, poured it all back into her heart and shoved it back into her open chest cavity. Again, barely putting in any effort, he started sewing her chest back shut. Most of the fluids dropped onto the floor or ran down her abdomen. He quickly and quite effortlessly finished sewing her chest shut and began to speak.

"Now finally, Era. We have picked apart your mind, We have analyzed your body. Now we can look into your soul."

These words excited Era. She began to jump in excitement, her top cranium bumping up and down. Her chest cavity stitches slowly coming undone from her heart sloshing around.

"How are we going to do that??" She excitedly asked.

The Sage responded, "Every time you dream, we'll be looking into your soul."

# Chapter 2

## Part 1

As Era woke up, she wondered what this day would bring her. What school would be, what lesson would add to her knowledge. What weather would cause the day to be like. How people she met would interact with her. What new lessons the Sage would teach when it was time to sleep.

The general studies degree she had chosen granted her an amalgam of classes to choose from. Today, for her 2$^{nd}$ day of college she would be taking a different class about psychology. This specific one being about a branch of psychology.

Era wondered if the things she learns in class will have an effect on her conversations with the Sage. Yesterday the Sage had told her that we are going to learn about every little aspect of who she is. But as she learned and grew, would this process in turn, be continual? She wasn't sure. She was lost in thought, pondering the Sage. Thinking about her dreams.

After getting ready and leaving her studio, she got to the building where her class was in. She went inside, sat down and waited on the professor. As she sat down, she giddily took out the contents of her backpack, placing her note taking equipment in front of her, ready to begin. Students came in slowly at first, sitting down, some repeating what

Era had just done. As the clock got closer to the designated class start time, the students began to come in droves. Finally, it was time and the professor walked in. A tall man with grey hair and glasses.

"Good morning class", he said. "My name is Professor Barker. We'll quickly being going over the syllabus and then jump right into the class." He took out some papers to pass out and handed it to one of the students to start passing around. He also took out some binders and a large book that undoubtedly held his class teaching notes and the reading material for the students. As soon as everyone had a copy of the syllabus, he began going over it.

Quickly was an understatement. Roughly 40 seconds and he instructed the class to pull out their note taking equipment. Many of the students looked disappointed as if they were expecting a quick and easy class. Some looked nervous as they fumbled to gather their note taking equipment. Some looked indifferent, as if they had been through multiple of these types of professors.

Class seemed to end abruptly as the professor began to gather his things. "I hope I didn't overwhelm you with too much information on our first day of class!" he joked. Era looked down and saw an absolute mess of notes and various scribbles that would definitely take time to make sense of. Era caught glimpses of other students notes and was relieved to find that their notes were as chaotic as hers were, most even more so.

Despite being so bombarded by information, she felt content. She got exactly what she wanted and will soon be able to make sense of it all. Although her classmates seemed less than excited about all the information given. She wondered if she would meet the sage again and if they would talk about the things that she had learned today.

She gathered her things, neatly putting them into her backpack. The class all skittishly walked towards the exits of the class, but Era decided to sit for a while longer. Pondering on the concepts that the professor of environmental psychology had taught. She wondered if this was part of what the Sage taught. What environments and factors could be found in the dissected psyche of one's brain?

She glanced down at her notes that she had written down. "different people learn in different ways", "some children respond better to corporal punishment while others respond well to positive reinforcement", "trauma can have long lasting effects", "overcompensation could be a result of past neglect or abuse". All of these were paraphrased sentences due to Era not being able to keep up with the professor's continuous onslaught of information. She thought more and glanced back at her notes. Then she thought more, glanced down again, thought more, getting lost in the concepts until the next class starting coming in. She decided to let it go and move on.

She picked up her backpack, headed towards the exit, then the building exit and began walking towards her car. The thoughts of environmental factors still on her mind she couldn't help but start taking note on each little environmental detail of the area where she was walking.

She felt a gentle breeze that threw up her jet-black hair. The breeze felt nice. It made its way to a small patch of dandelions, causing the seeds to scatter. Some landing not too far away, and some being carried up into the sky and out of Eras line of sight, never to be seen again.

She continued walking and glanced down at some Roses that had been placed along the sidewalk for decoration. Roses that students would occasionally stop to admire and smell. One student tried to pick one but didn't realize that they had thorns. As soon as her fingers touched the stem, the thorns pierced her fingertips, and she immediately withdrew her hand, wincing in pain. The group she was walking with laughed at her and she laughed along with them.

She turned her head to some cacti that had also been placed near the sidewalks for decorative purposes. No Student would even attempt to try to touch these plants that were well known for their ability to cause harm.

The sunlight heating up Era's soft, tanned skin, she realized it was getting to the hottest part of the day and saw students taking refuge from the sun in various shaded areas. She didn't blame them. The gentle breeze was gone, and it was over 90 degrees at this point. She decided to join a small group of students in one of the shaded areas and take a small rest from her long walk. As she sat down and put her backpack down, she looked back at the little pieces of scenery and took it all in. After some time and resting, she took a deep breath and continued on.

She eventually made her way to her car and headed

home. She mentally took note of the little bits of scenery on every street corner, every stop light, every house, and every building. Bus stops with benches to allow people to rest. Houses with tire swings on trees, some with broken windows and beat up ceilings. Building that served the purpose of driver's registration or stores. But most importantly, a building that housed the gym she used to train at. She was anxious to get back to her training.

Eventually getting to her small studio apartment and letting her thoughts on the day fester in her curious brain. She studied for a few hours and made sense of her notes. Rather than a chaotic slew of words and scribbles, she retook them and organized them in a clear and concise manner. The process also allowed her to make sense of her jumbled thoughts.

After she had finished studying, she decided to treat herself with some physical activity. "To train the mind you must train the body." The words of her old coach resonated with Era even years later. She couldn't do her desired routine, but she could make do with what she had. Some dumbbells up to 40 pounds and a barbell. She's made do with less as a child. She changed into some exercise attire. A sports bra, spandex pants, and some light running shoes.

She began getting the blood in her muscles flowing. Warming up before the actual workout itself. Dynamic stretches for about 10 minutes. Then onto the routine itself. She grabbed some lightweight dumbbells and began shadow boxing. A 1,2 combo. 1,2,3 combo. Slip, slip. slip, right hook. 1,1,2,3. Jab, jab, uppercut. All the basic combos her old coach told her to work on to keep her skills up to par. After a few minutes of shadow boxing, she cranked out 50 pushups. At her peak she could do 100 without breaking a sweat. Next were some light curls with the 30-pound dumbbells. Then squats, then overhead press. After 10 minutes she started to develop a sweat. Another 10 minutes passed, and she started noticing a vein popping out of her defined bicep with every curl. And some light burning in her thick quadriceps with every squat. Sweat glistening off of her lightly defined abs. She loved these feelings. Training was something no one could ever take away from her. It was a form of control.

After 45 minutes, she decided to stop and stretch. Typical yoga poses to prevent injury and promote recovery. Lost in the heaven that is physical training, Era began reflecting on the classes again. After some time, she decided to shower and get ready to sleep early so she could wake up early.

She ate her typical lean meats and vegetables for health and fitness but allowed herself some sweet bread. Then she headed to the restroom to shower. Steam covering the mirror from her chosen shower heat of hell, she continued pondering on the classes. Every so often returning to the thought of getting back to training. She exited and put on her usual sleeping attire. Her hair still damp and spiked at the end. Era checked to make sure that she had everything she needed to start the day in the morning.

After verifying, she finished drying her hair and eventually laid down. Her head hit the pillow and she quickly drifted away into a deep sleep.

# Part 2

## "This is my garden. This is how I grow."

Era found herself in wide-open fields, with various patches of different weather and different terrain. Almost as if each little patch had its own little ecosystem governed by a different spirit. Like she was looking into the minds of an entire crowd of people.

A hand was gently placed on her shoulder. Era turned to see the familiar mask worn face of her teacher. She couldn't help but feel a sense of power coming from the Sage. Yet, he felt welcoming and endearing. The gloves he was wearing were padded at the knuckles and as black as Eras spike tipped hair.

"Hello, Era. It's nice to see you again." Said the Sage with an unseeable smile on his mask-worn face. "What do you see here in these lands?"

As Era looked into this new dreamscape, she was amazed. Different patches of land all with varying overhead weather and scenery. She saw a desert filled with sand and blistering sunlight, a patch of green plains with some small clouds overhead. But before she finished looking, she felt the Sage squeeze her shoulder, telling her to answer him.

"I see a lot of different patches of vegetation. Each with

different weather overhead. Some with clouds, some with rain, each one is different." Replied Era.

"Very perceptive.", The Sage congratulated. "Let's go see up close."

They both began to walk closer to one of the patches. As she got closer, she began to see the specific forms of vegetation in each patch. Some beautiful, overshadowed with pristine weather, some ugly and beaten down with harsh weather.

They arrived at one of the patches and look closely. It was a bed of roses. An absolutely beautiful bed of light red Roses. Era could feel a warm sunlight from the sky and breathed in the fresh rain smell that had just passed. The ground smelled full of nutrients so these Roses could grow quickly and healthy. But as Era tried to pick one up, the Sage of Darkness stopped her.

"Wait, Era." the Sage calmly warned.

"These Roses have thorns that will quickly puncture your skin."

Era looked and saw the thorns deceptively hiding right beneath the petals and leaves of the Rose. And she realized the danger of attempting to grab something so beautiful with such haste.

"These Roses have such a lovely environment. Given all the sun and water they could need to grow so beautiful. But that doesn't mean they cannot hurt you."

"But without the love that this environment gives them, these roses would not have been able to grow at all." replied Era.

"That is correct." Said the Sage. "This is the nature of the Rose. This is the way this flower grows."

The two began to walk towards the next patch of vegetation. As they entered, Era was suddenly bombarded with an intense heat and blistering sun. She couldn't help but wince and shield her face from the relentless light. She noticed the ground was loose and difficult to walk on, and she quickly realized that this was a patch of desert.

As she slowly adjusted and opened her eyes, she saw some cacti. Tall and powerful Cacti that towered over her and the Sage. She walked towards the cactus titans and waited for the Sage to speak.

"I'm sure I don't have to tell you not to touch these." Chuckled the Sage.

"Well duh." Scoffed Era.

She looked intently at the cactus, trying to think what the Sage may say and said, "These cacti are given next to nothing. Yet they are strong and able to grow in the harshest of environments. Actually, it looks like these cacti REQUIRE a harsh environment. Plus, with their thorns, hardly anything can get close to it. Is this the nature of the cactus?"

"Yes." Confirmed the sage. "But that doesn't mean that they cannot be beautiful, as well." He pointed towards the top of one of the cacti. And Era saw a gorgeous flower growing despite the blistering, harsh conditions.

The two moved on towards the next patch. As they moved into this new patch, Era was welcomed with a gust of cool wind. This new patch wasn't consistent with itself at all. Some areas were damp and humid, some were sandy, and some even had bits of trash in it. The only thing that Era could see that had any level of consistency was the sight of thousands of dandelions.

The sage began to speak as Era was still trying to gather her thoughts.

"Dandelions can grow just about anywhere. Whether it is a harsh environment, or a giving environment. But the only way they'll reproduce is with this wind carrying on the seeds to new places. This is the nature of the dandelion."

The Sage continued, "You see Era? Different environments produce different flowers. Different vegetation. Just like people. Some people need a harsh environment, just like the cactus so that they may become strong. Some people need love and care, like the rose. Some people will grow wherever in abundance like the dandelion, as long as you give them their freedom."

Era began to wonder. She looked at her hands and asked, "What kind of flower am I?"

The Sage nodded his head in gesture to move forward to the next patch. They both turned and walked. And as they walked into the next patch, the sun disappeared. The moon and starlight filled the sky. Era looked down and saw a flutter of yellow and pink flowers that blossomed as the darkness filled the night sky.

As Era admired the beauty of this unknown flower, the Sage began to speak.

"The moonflower, Era." He answered. "You blossom in the darkness."

# Chapter 3

## Part 1

A few months had passed, and Era had developed a good routine for her current work life. Balancing school, a part time job, and even staying physically fit. She had unexpectedly taken well to her job as a teacher's assistant. She wasn't sure how the primary school kids would receive her before she started but they took a liking to her. She had also recently decided to go back to training at her old gym and was excited to see her old coach.

After one of her classes, she decided to discuss some things with one of the professors. Some of the other students did as well, forming a small line behind Era. The professor seemed to be mildly annoyed at the questions that the students were all asking, as he was constantly repeating himself.

After finishing her conversation with the professor, Era turned to head out of the classroom. As she did, she noticed two particular students looking at her. A squirrely looking girl with glasses and long wiry hair looking absolutely exhausted. And another skinny, sweaty looking boy glancing at her boobs, immediately correcting himself as Era looked at him.

"H-h-heeyy…" Said the girl with glasses.

Era stopped.

"Can… can I ask you something?" Queried the girl.

"Umm, yeah. What's up?" Said Era.

"You work, right? I've seen you at my younger sister's school before." Said the girl.

"Yes, I do, why?" Answered Era.

"And… you work out too, right? I mean, you have a great figure. You're more muscular than most of the men in these classes." Asked the girl.

"Yes? I… used to compete in boxing. I'm actually going back to my old gym soon." Era answered while scratching her head, not knowing what to do with her hands. She wondered where this girl was going with all of this.

The girl continued, "How do you do it?"

Era paused and gave her what-the-actual-fuck look. Puckered lips and squinted eyes. "What do you mean?" She asked.

"Well, you're doing so well in the class. You have one of the best grades out of all of us. Plus, you work, and still have time to exercise. I can barely keep up with the pace of these classes and I'm feeling overwhelmed with the little part time job I have. I would like to start exercising but can't find the time or energy. And I was wondering what your secret is?"

Era awkwardly smiled and replied, "Weeellll… I just really like exercising. That's how I spend my free time. As far as school and work goes. Uhm… I don't really know how to explain it. I think attitude and how you handle stress is a big part of it. That's what my coach taught me."

"Oh… ok…", Said the girl. "I just… I can't. I… I just feel like these classes are suffocating me. I have to do everything the professors say, and I feel the weight of the stress just getting to me. And this voice in the back of my head says I have to do this or else I'll end up jobless."

Era began sympathizing with the girl and awkwardly put her hand on her shoulder. She didn't really know what to say but tried speaking some words of encouragement anyways.

"All I can say is work hard, believe in yourself, and never give up!" Era said while grinning ear to ear. It wasn't the most awkward thing she had ever said, but it was definitely up there.

The girl let out a little tear. "Th-…Thank you." She choked as she wiped a tear off her cheek.

As Era took her hand off her shoulder, the young girls wallet feel out of her purse, exposing her student ID. It read "Anabel Sollicitus".

Era smiled at Anabel and started walking towards the exit. As she walked past the boy shamelessly looking at her boobs, she caught a scent of beer. And sex. The young man raised his eyes and gave a pathetic attempt at a come-hither smile. Era rolled her eyes in disgust.

"Ugh. Boys." She thought to herself.

As she headed out the exit of the building, Era realized how much the time she spent talking to that girl and the professor took. She was running a bit behind for work. She started jogging to her car to make up for lost time, hopped in and headed to the primary school she worked at.

A quick 5-minute drive later, she arrived. She put on her lanyard that identified her as a teachers aid and walked inside. She was scheduled to arrive to help right after the kids had lunch and recess. All the kids were already sitting down as she walked in, and they all burst into excitement.

"MISS ERA! MISS ERA! MISS ERA!!" The kids all screamed.

A short middle-aged woman with heavy hips and a pixie haircut briefly stopped teaching and welcomed Era. She wore brown leggings, and a loose orange shirt.

"Hi, Era!" Miss Magist said. "Could you help Rusty again? He's in one of his moods and won't talk."

Era looked at a desk at the end of the row in the back of the classroom. And there sat a little boy, looking sad. His arms were crossed, and he had long scruffy hair, as if it hadn't been cut in months. His pale skin insinuated he didn't spend much time in the sun, and his young face was covered in unwashed skin.

Era walked over, pulled up a chair and sat down next to him. "What's wrong, Rusty?" Asked Era.

The boy just sat in silence, looking down. Era knew that something had probably happened at his house again.

Young Rusty would often confide in Era about his home life. Broken bottles, yelling, and some bruised faces were a very frequent part of this boy's life. And this youngling was constantly getting into fights to vent his frustration. And Era knew all too well what this was like, so she took a special interest in him. "Did something happen, Rusty?"

"MY NAME IS RUSTICA!!" Screamed the boy. The noise took the entire class by surprise and interrupted what Miss Magist was teaching. Era briefly lost her temper and grabbed the boy by his arm and dragged him outside. After they were both in the hallways, Era squatted down and grabbed the boy by both of his arms and shook him a little.

"RUSTY!! YOU DON'T SCREAM LIKE THAT IN THE MIDDLE OF CLASS. HOW MANY TIMES DO I HAVE TO TELL YOU?" Era quietly but sternly told him.

The boy winced and let out a small tear. Era realized she had gone a bit overboard and loosened her grip.

Era tried to calm down. She took a deep breath and asked again. "What's wrong, Rusty?"

Rusty finally answered. "The other kids keep making fun of my hair. I asked my dad to take me to get it cut, but he's always sleeping. And I haven't seen my mom in forever."

"It's ok, Rust." Reassured Era. "I'll see if I can take you this weekend. Is that ok?"

After hearing Era's proposition, young Rusty's face lit up. "Really Miss Era!! Thaank yoou!!" He said while throwing his arms around her neck.

The two went back inside and continued on with the class. Typical basic reading lessons and arithmetic. The class all seemed to learn a bit quicker with Era around. Probably because they were mildly afraid of her.

The school day ended, and Era headed to her car. "BYE MISS ERA!" Rusty yelled as he walked home. Era smiled and said goodbye, hoping his home life will start improving after the child shielding agency gets involved.

After a substantial period of time away from her training, Era was finally headed back. Now able to integrate it after finding a good school-work balance. She knew she'd be exhausted afterwards, but her house was a two-minute drive away. The entire reason she had chosen that specific studio apartment.

She drove to her old gym to meet up with her old coach. Double checking to make sure she had her equipment; she walked in and was immediately greeted with a warm smile. A tall, dark skinned 200-pound man with a slender, yet thick build and black twined hair in the style of a flat top.

"ERA!!" Her old coach Cassius exclaimed. "Haven't seen ya in a few months, girly! Finally decidin' to work on going semi?"

Era chuckled and replied, "I'm not sure about trying to go semi, but I at least want to get back in shape. I'm in school and I have work, coach. Remember?"

Cassius smiled and put his arm on Era's shoulder. "I figured as much, kiddo. But to be frank, thas all fuckin bullshit. You could be well on yo way to being a top-class fighter in your weight class! Why you wastin' it on this college nonsense?"

"I just wanna work on my mind too, coach. I'm not saying I won't try going pro, I just would like to educate myself as well. My parents didn't' have any type of school and I don't want to end up like them."

Cassius smiled. "Well, ok girly. If ya' say so. Let's get your account set back up. Y'know the drill."

Era went to the familiar receptionist and began all the paperwork.

"So, what is your schedule like?" Asked Cassius. "How often will you be training?"

"Honestly, coach. Not a lot. A full schedule of classes and part time work will keep me pretty busy. Plus, I'd really like to try being more social for once in my life."

Cassius laughed. "No shit? So, yur finally tryin to break outta of yur loner phase, huh? You wouldn't even talk to your teammates, let alone come to any team events. I guess ya really are tryin' to grow. This will be good for you when ya have press conferences and cameras shuttering all around you." Cassius was ever relentless in his desire for Era to go pro.

"Thanks, coach. I'll try to come in at least 3 times a week for 1 hour. 2 if possible. Just enough to keep me in shape. And I won't forget about trying to go semi as I'm in college. Deal?"

"Deal!" Cassius said with a hopeful smile.

They got right into it after the contract was all worked out Era changed over into her usual training attire and began their usual routine. Form work, slip drills, combos, power hooks, uppercuts, and more. After their drill Cassius had her do some high intensity interval training full of pushups, curls, jump ropes, box jumps and many more. Era was worried that she would slip on the sweat that she left on the floor.

"TIME!!" Said Cassius, signaling the end of the final round.

Era took a deep breath and dropped to her knees, then falling onto her hands. Sopping in sweat, a steady stream of drops fell from her nose. Her hair spiked at the end from being wet.

"A lil outa shape, huh?" Cassius said with a chuckle.

Era got off her hands, looked at her coach, smiled, and signaled with her hands: 'Just a lil'.

"It won't take me too long to get back into my flow, coach." Said Era. "I've actually been doing the routine you gave me to keep me in decent shape.

"Glad to hear it!" Said Cassius. "Aight now get outta here, I have to close up!"

Era did as she was told. She quickly showered, changed,

and headed out. Feeling in a good mood, Era decided to swing by the bar. She hadn't been there in a while, but thought she deserved a bit of indulging after such a productive day.

She drove over to the 'Black Elysium' and parked her car.

'I wonder if he's working today.' Era thought.

Era stepped out of her car, headed to the door, walked in, and sat at her Usual spot. A short stalky man was there in place of the other bartender boy, but he was busy serving other customers. Feeling slightly disappointed, Era looked up to read the possible drink she would order from the menu screen.

Suddenly the back door swung open, and that familiar face quickly made its way to the main bar.

"Sorry I'm late, man!" The bartender boy apologized. "Thanks for covering for me!"

The short stalky man turned around. "Yur always late ya fuckin idiot."

The Bartender just smiled. "Yeeaaahhh, school is rough man."

The short bartender rolled his eyes and headed out the back door. He looked at Era and smiled.

"Hey! I remember you!" He said.

Era let out a faint smile, not really knowing what to say.

"I've seen you around campus, but you're always walking too quick for me to say anything! Do you go to school part time or full?"

Era lightly swallowed and answered. "I go full time, getting my general studies degree. What about you?"

"Oh, I'm still just getting my basics. But I'm pretty set on getting my degree in physics so I can be a researcher. So, what do you want this time? Another screwdriver?" The bartender boy asked.

"Wellll… can't really go wrong with that." Era said.

The bartender boy quickly and skillfully made Era her drink. He served her and they started talking for a while. As Era became more intoxicated, she felt her face warming up and becoming slightly more confident. Slowly, all the other customers made their way out and it was just the two of them.

"That's crazy, I've never met a woman who boxes before." He said. "I used to compete a little in grappling. I also was on my schools swim team as a teenager, but can't find time to get back into it with school and work." He looked up at the clock and realized it was closing time.

"Oooo sorry. I need to start closing up. "Apologized the bartender boy while giving charming sideways smile.

"It's ok." Said Era. "I should probably head home soon, anyways."

Era picked up her things and began heading out the

door. She could hear the bartender boy starting to put things away and noticed the lights going out one by one. She placed her hand on the door, but before she opened it, she heard his voice call her.

"Hey!" He asked. "What's your name, anyways? I don't quite remember from class."

"It's Era." She answered. "Yours?"

"Eros Amare." He answered back. "My friends call me Arrow."

Era smiled and waved goodbye as she opened the door and left. She hopped in her car and headed home. 'Eros Amare', she thought while picturing his tall body and sideways smile and blushing. The alcohol was making her think a little differently than usual.

"Probably had a bit too much to drive, but I live close." She thought to herself.

After a short drive, she arrived at her studio apartment. Having a slight buzz and being exhausted from the day, Era decided that she would waste no time heading to her bed.

Era walked through her door and took a quick glance around her studio apartment. She had posters of her college, Jannah University. With a split moon as its logo. A recently hung-up brochure of Elysium Pub hanging from her wall, with crossing swords behind a beer glass as it's logo.

Era quickly changed, threw her things on the floor and

threw herself onto her bed. She looked at the nightstand next to her and saw a picture of her and Miss Magist posing for a picture with the younglings. A sign in front read 'Svarga primary school'. And next to it, a picture of her and Coach Cassius, fists up, posing for a picture with the gym logo 'HV' behind them.

She turned over and closed her eyes. "Let's see what'll happen this time." Era thought before she drunkenly swirled into a deep sleep.

# Part 2

## "A stranger's perspective"

Era found herself in a city this time. A city she has never been to, but for some reason felt comfortable in it. She didn't see the Sage so decided to walk until she found him. She walked the unfamiliar streets for a while, looking for the Sage until she eventually found him sightseeing, looking up and taking pictures with a small camera. It was odd to see the Sage so taken back and enamored by the buildings and fountains.

"What the hell? Are you sightseeing??" Chuckled Era. "I wouldn't really expect you to be into that kind of thing. Especially since you've been here before. You look a lil' silly gazing up at building and taking pictures with your mask on."

"This place is as new to me as it is to you." The Sage calmly replied. "As were the gardens and the laboratories."

Era raised her eyebrow and tilted her head. "How are these places new to you? You knew everything about them and have been showing me these things and places as if you lived here all your life?"

"And I have." Stated the Sage.

Era gave her 'what the actual fuck' look, puckering her lips, squinting her eyes, and shook her head in confusion and exhaled to blow her hair out of her face. But before she could let out more of her frazzled words, the Sage interrupted. "Don't worry about it, follow me."

It really was a beautiful city. High rise buildings, with not a single piece of trash on the floor. Intricate designs and dazzling lights. Flowing fountains and small canals. Yet no people around. They kept walking in silence until they came across a familiar sight.

Era's college, Jannah University. It was mildly poetic that the Sage would teach her something in a place that she was consistently learning from already. But she was excited. They eventually walked their way to one of her classrooms and saw a professor standing there at the podium. The teacher had no face, nor a voice, but somehow, she knew it was ONE of her professors.

The professor walked up to the Sage, and they shook hands. Then the Sage began to raise his hands towards the face of the professor. Era somehow knew exactly what he was doing. And for some reason, she was compelled to act at the same time. She also knew what she needed to do.

Era took her two eyes out and held them out for the

Sage to take. At the same time, the Sage took the eyes from the professor's skull. Taking Era's eyes out of her hand and placing the professors in them instead, Era inserted these new eyes into her head.

She opened her eyes and looked around the classroom. But instead of seeing desks and chairs, she saw cribs and mobiles. And the walls were all coated with cartoon characters and silly drawings. Stifling her laughter, she looked towards a window and saw a reflection of herself and drew a blank face. Her reflection was that of a 3-year-old baby with a dumb look on its face.

"What the fuck is this?" Era scoffed.

"You have his eyes. This is the way the professor sees this place. This is his perception." Said the Sage.

"You have got to be fucking shittin' me!" Era sternly said. "So, he sees me as a literal baby?! That's fucking bullshit!"

The Sage shook his head while giving a light chuckle. "He just thinks the younger people are immature and whine a lot. But considering you're throwing a fit, he's not too far off, is he?"

Era took the professors eyes out and stuck them out with her hand. "Just give me back my frikin eyes, please. Geezus." The Sage complied and gave her eyes back.

"Ok, now what?" Era said, visibly annoyed.

"I don't know what you're giving me attitude for, the

Professor is the one that views you like that, not me." The Sage laughed.

Era rolled her eyes.

"Alright, now let's walk to the next room." Said the Sage.

The two walked into a different classroom and found two of her classmates. She couldn't see their face or any distinguishable characteristics, but she knew they were classmates. One a male and the other a female.

The Sage began taking the eyes out of the female classmate first as Era proceeded to take out her eyes again. Finishing the switch, she opened her eyes.

She saw the classroom take the form of a prison. With rules and warnings plastered all over the walls of the room. Some of the rules reading "COMPLY" and other reading things like "YOUR LIFE IS IN OUR HANDS" and "WORK UNTIL YOU DIE". She saw students walking around with chains everywhere and covered in black and white striped clothing. Era became sad that this was her classmates perception, wondering how much stress she has been going through. She then looked at the window to see her reflection. She took the form of a soft faced woman, older than she was. Free of chains and wearing a crown on her head.

"Huh. So, this girl sees me like this?" Questioned Era.

"Yes, answered the Sage. "She sees you handling everything so well that you aren't shackled the way everyone else is. And she sees you as an absolute queen."

Era blushed a bit, held her hands to her cheeks and let out a little squeal. "EEEEE I'M SO FLATTERED."

The Sage let out a small chuckle. That won't last very long." Said the Sage as he reached out to switch out eyes with the male student. The two quickly switched and Era opened her eyes to see something ridiculous. Party banners everywhere, kegs, condoms on the floor, and loudspeakers blaring music.

"Really?" said Era. "College isn't a fucking party scene. Ugh." She reluctantly looked at a mirror to see her reflection in a window. Instantly blushing furiously red, she clenched her teeth while her hair turned upward, and she let out a light gasp. Her reflection was definitely her own. But with a short miniskirt, a visible thong, a tank top 4 sizes too small for her with a bullseye logo on it, and boobs twice as big as the ones she had.

"OH MY GOD!!! ARE YOU FUCKING!! KIDDING ME RIGHT NOW?!" Screamed Era. "YOU CANNOT BE SERIOUSLY!!!"

The Sage was visibly holding back his laughter with a balled-up fist held up to the mouth portion of his mask. "Some people will see you like this. It's unavoidable." The Sage said while stifling his laughter.

"UGH!! I prefer to be seen as a fucking infant instead of this fucking… THING!"

"At least he thinks you're hot." Chuckled the Sage as he

reached out for the eyes. "He could have thought you were flat chested and ugly with no sense of style."

"UGH WHATEVER!", Screeched Era. She put her own eyes back in and glared at the Sage until they moved on to the next location.

"The Sage was still visibly laughing as they both walked out of the classroom to the next destination. Era was huffing and blushing the entire way, highly insulted but somewhat flattered, though she'd never admit it.

After a short time of walking, they made it to a small familiar school. It was the school where Era worked as a teacher's aid. Svarga primary school. The wheels started turning and Era began to guess who's eyes the Sage was going to give to her. They made their way to the playground and there, a child stood playing on the jungle gym.

It was the same little boy that Era had noticed since she started working there. Rusty. The little boy jumped off the jungle gym and ran towards the Sage and hugged him. The Sage kneeled, patted the youngling on the head and took out his eyes. Era and the Sage once again swapped.

Era opened her eyes to see everything much larger than a second ago. Some other kids showed up and took the form as little gremlins that would screech and point at her. The banners and signs on the walls of the school went from legible to incomprehensible symbols. Era walked towards a puddle and looked down to see her own reflection. She had taken somewhat of a monstrous and excessively muscular appearance. A scary and intense look in her eyes, almost glowing, with a tag on her shirt that read 'Miss Era'. It was written in the same handwriting as the young boy and Era realized it was the same as the way she taught the little boy to write her name.

"So, the little boy is scared of the world and sees me as something monstrous??" Asked Era.

"It's not just that. He sees you as something that actually makes sense in a world where he only sees chaos. Albeit, scary. That's why your name is very legible, unlike the rest of the signs and posters around here." Era looked at her reflection again and sighed heavily. She then returned the eyes, and they left the playground. As they walked away, Era began feeling disappointed in herself.

"Now how about someone you've been familiar with for years, Era?" Asked the Sage.

"Sure, why not?" Era replied.

The two left the playgrounds of the school and began walking down the street. Era noticed that the streets now had people. All with very distinct eyes. She occasionally noticed the expression that one of these had on their face but didn't pay it any heed.

After some time walking, they came up to a very familiar building. One that filled her with pure joy. Era's gym, HallaVall Martial arts, where she trains with coach Cassius. Era immediately ran into the building to look for her coach. She saw him doing some his signature shuffle in the boxing ring. Her coach saw her, stopped, and exited the ring while walking towards her.

After a short while, the Sage caught up to Era. Cassius saw the Sage and the two walked up to each other and gave a warm hug.

"I know you were excited to see how your coach sees you, but you didn't have to ditch me like that." Said the Sage as he reached out to take the eyes of Cassius.

"I knowwww, but I'm so excited to know how he sees meee!!" Squealed Era as she removed her eyes and held them out.

After she placed Cassius' eyes in her skull, she opened them and quickly ran to the mirror used for shadow boxing to get a good look at herself. She was torn between mild insult and an endearing warmth.

Her reflection was that of a much younger version of herself, around 13. Much younger than she is now, wearing multiple belts with her old gloves and headgear on.

"It's been a while since I fought, but it hasn't been THAAAAT long." Said Era. "And I only had 1 belt! From when I was 16! Not that many!"

"Maybe not." Said the Sage. "But your coach still sees you as young. And full of potential.

Era kept looking at her reflection as the Sage spoke. "it's not an insult that he sees you as young, he's just an older person. A coach should see their protégés as young and full of potential. It's actually a compliment to perceive you in this way."

Era let out a huge goofy grin and a little tear. She removed her coaches eyes, and the two walked out of the gym, headed to the next spot.

Era and the Sage walked in silence. Passing the various buildings on the sides of the streets, but this time there were more people. A lot, actually. Each with a very distinct look in their eyes. And this time, Era took note of each one. Some looked at her with derision, some with contempt, some with lust, and some with indifference. Some eyes looked the same, but some had a very distinct look. That all too familiar look of dogmatic judgment.

"I'm sure you're noticing by now, Era." Said the Sage. Everyone will view you differently. And you can actually learn a lot about yourself if you look at yourself from another person's perspective. The professor views you and the students as young and immature, but there's a reason for it. All of you are, and you all need to grow up. Those students view you very differently, but knowing others see you as well-put-together and attractive means you're doing things right and can help your self-esteem. That little boy viewing you as something so scary probably means you need to work on making yourself a little more welcoming, considering you're working with kids. Your coach sees you as young and full of potential because you are."

Era raised her hand to her and bit her fingernails. She didn't realize she had been so intimidating and immature. But she took a modicum of solace knowing her peers saw her as something mostly positive. And most heartwarming of all, her coach seeing her the way he did. She then realized that her perception of others is very telling about herself.

After a long period of time walking and many eyes being seen, and a lot of thinking, they finally arrived to the final destination. A still somewhat new and unfamiliar but warm place.

The Bar that Eros Amare worked at. The Black Elysium. She looked up at the Sage and he looked down to her. Surely another interesting lesson would take place here, but she couldn't help but wonder what lesson the Sage could teach her at a place of debauchery. They both walked inside and saw the bartender cleaning glasses at the main counter. The bartender boy seemed a bit taller and more handsome than in real life. Era felt her face warm up as the Sage slowly walked towards the Bartender boy. The Bartender boy came around stood in front of the Sage and gave him his eyes. The Sage went up to Era and reached out his hand that held the eyes. Era reached for them and put them in her skull. She slowly opened her eyes and as her vision came into focus, the first thing she saw was the numbers on her alarm clock as the alarm rang and rang.

# Chapter 4

## Part 1

Era's next few months at school went by quickly, as she began to become acclimated to her routine more and more. From college, to work, to training. This semester was near its end. She would sometimes take time in between classes to go over her notes, study and take in whatever information she had been going though in her various classes to ensure she would pass her finals with flying colors.

Today, she decided to go to the commons area to do some light studying. As she opened up one of the chairs and set her backpack down, she heard someone start bawling.

She turned her head and saw a younger man right behind her. With his head on the table, gasping in between his yells of anguish. There was an opened computer right in front of him. A young woman sitting next to him began patting him on the back while giving words of comfort.

Era glanced at the opened computer and noticed an email with a "Notice of failure to pass required class" in its subject. Era knew about the school policies and that failures of required classes meant that someone has failed too many classes and would be required to drop out.

Era had noticed this young man before. In the same commons area before, he always had this defeated look on his face while he attempted to study. The same face that Era had worn as a young teenager, after failing in everything that she had tried before. Hands pulling her hair, almost on the verge of tears, looking down with dead eyes. It seemed that this young man has let it all get to him as she did back then.

The young man tried to stifle his crying and proceeded to gather his things while he talked with his friend that was trying to console him. Era turned her head to face the table she was at and opened her backpack, taking out her notes. She put some headphones in, and set down the notes from her recently finished class. The instructor was from a foreign country called Sweetzerland, Professor Carl. The class was over something called "shadow work". A vaguely familiar concept, Era wrote down every word of the lecture she possibly could and tried to reorganize them in a way that made more sense to her.

Some time had passed by and Era glanced down at her watch to see an hour had passed. Time to go to work. She gathered her things and headed back to the school. Today, after lunch the kids were to give a short show-and-tell. Era had been helping Rusty with his show and tell and was excited to see him show everything off.

Era showed up a little earlier than usual, and caught sight of the younglings playing on the playground for their recess.

"MISS ERA! MISS ERA!!" Yelled a little boy while running towards her.

Rusty's happy little face caused Era to smile ear to ear. "HI RUSTY!"

"Miss Era! Are we gon do show n tell today?" Rusty asked.

"Yes, sir! Are you excited? Do you remember what you're going to show?", Era answered.

"Mhhmmm Im gonna show my drawings from the peektures you showed me." Rusty said.

Era had noticed Rusty liked to draw during recess and during free time so she had decided she would bring him some Art to imitate. And when Miss Magist told the class they would be doing a show and tell, Era tried helping Rusty plan on showing the class his drawings.

"Good, Rusty." Era said she patted him on the head. "Now go play, and I'll see you inside."

"Okay!!" Rusty yelled as he ran off to continue his little drawings. He had been working on the drawings nonstop every day for weeks, and was clearly focused on making them good and showing them off for show and tell

Era headed inside to meet Miss Magist and they began getting the little stage ready for the kids.

"So, how's school?" Asked Miss Magist. "Passing all your classes?"

"I'm actually SMASHING all my classes." Era bragged. "I'm still not sure what I can do with a general studies degree, tho. I'm kinda worried."

"I'm sure you'll figure something out." Reassured Miss Magist. "You have a pretty good way of dealing with things."

"Thank you… Ama..?." Said Era, letting out a light nervous chuckle. "Still getting used to calling you by your first name."

"You'll get used to it, Era. And it's pronounced 'Amantes'" Said Miss Magist with a smile.

The two shared a lighthearted chuckle as the kids came in. Recess was over and it was time to begin the show and tell. The kids all scurried to their desks, sat down and began pulling out their little items to show.

"Now." Said Miss Magist. "Who wants to go first?"

Several children hands shot straight into the air, eager to go. Era glanced around the room and noticed Rusty was looking down, seemingly reluctant to raise his hands.

Miss Magist picked one of the children and one by one they all made their presentations. Most chose to show pictures of their pet and animals, some read from their favorite children's books, some even showed some science experiments they thought was fun. But as each one went, Era noticed Rusty receding further and further into his chair. Finally, the last youngling went and only Rusty was left.

"Ok, Rusty." Said Miss Magist. "Your turn!"

But Rusty stayed in his chair looking down.

"C'mon Rusty! Your turn!" Miss Magist repeated.

All the kids turned their eyes to Rusty. As their piercing, judgmental child eyes looked at him, Rusty picked up his feet to his chair, hugged his knees, and looked down even further.

"Rusty." Miss Magist sternly said. "I'm not going to tell you again."

Era began to become annoyed. She had spent a lot of time with him to help him with his show and tell. Finding him pictures that she thought he could imitate, looking up ways to help kids with art, helping him pick out what drawings he would show and how he would show them.

She quickly walked over to his desk put her hand on his shoulder, moved close to his ears and aggressively whispered, "Rusty. You had better get your ASS over there and do your show and tell. This is NOT acceptable!"

Rusty's eyes began to water as he hugged his knees tighter. Era's temper flared up and she grabbed him by the arm to pick him up. He wiped away his tears and slowly walked towards the little stage in front of the class. He opened up his backpack and took out his drawings. He took a weak hearted stance, feet together, slumped shoulders, and eyes facing down. He held one of them up, A beautiful sketch of a forest.

"T-this… isa… forest…" He stuttered as he shifted to another picture. A well-done sketch of a cliff overlooking the sea.

"A-a-and… t-this… i-…isa… ocean…" He stuttered.

The cruel class of children began laughing at him and he reached down to put his drawings away and slipped, dropping his other drawings. Causing the class to laugh even louder.

"Quiet!!" Yelled Miss Magist. "We don't laugh at others, is that understood??"

The class went silent as Era walked towards Rusty to help him gather his things. He had 2 drawings left. A dense metropolitan city full of dazzling lights, fancy signs, and intricate high-rise buildings. And another of a peaceful suburban area.

Era shooed Rusty back to his desk and Miss Magist began lecturing the class until the bell finally rang. She dismissed the class, and all the kids left the classroom. Era stayed back to help Miss Magist clean up.

"A little harsh with Rusty, Era." Said Miss Magist as she took apart the little stage.

"Ugh. I just. I just wanted him to do good on his show and tell. He'd been working so hard, and I was helping him!!" Era replied.

"Yea." Said Miss Magist. "It's a shame what fear can do to a person, let alone a child."

Her words struck a chord with Era and the two locked eyes. Era realized what Miss Magist was trying to tell her and she looked down in shame.

"I'll finish up here, Era. You can go home."

Era accepted the offer and gathered her stuff to head out. Despite the shame of the unspoken lecture given to her by Miss Magist, she felt excited to train today. One of those rare days where she would be able to spar for training. She walked out of the classroom, got into her car, and headed towards the gym.

A short drive later, she was in the parking lot. She hurried inside, changed into her usual attire, and began warming up in preparation. While she was calmly working some light combos on the heavy bag, she saw Cassius talking to one of the younger rookies. The rookie was wearing her headgear already and seemed to be scared of the upcoming sparring.

"There she is!" Cassius greeted as Era approached them. "Hey, Era!"

"Sup' coach." Said Era. "Who am I sparring today?"

Cassius wrapped his arm around the young rookie. "Right here, girly. She needs someone experienced to help show her weaknesses without beating her up too much."

Era let out a small laugh. "You sure, coach? She seems pretty scared."

Cassius laughed in response. "Exactly why, girly. She needs to control her fear in the face of someone much better so she can grow."

Cassius faced the young rookie and put both his hands

on her shoulders. "Lemme tell you something that my ole' coach Constantine taught me. He told me that fear isn' a bad thing. It's something that we can control. Nature gave us fear, and if we can understand it, we can manipulate it and it can make us better. Do ya understand?"

The young rookie nervously nodded her head. "Now go head' and gettin the ring." Said Cassius. He turned his head to look at Era. "You too, girly."

The two both climbed in the ring. Era was a couple inches taller than the rookie, even with her headgear on. Era chose not to put hers on, not expecting to have much of a challenge from someone shorter and weighed roughly 30 pounds less that her.

Cassius took the young rookies corner and whispered some instruction to her as Era began jumping leg to leg to hype herself up for one of the things she loves to do most.

"Aight, Era! Don' beat er up too bad! Just keep her on er toes!" Cassius yelled to Era from across the ring. Era nodded her head to signify compliance and the bell rang.

Both of them walked to the center of the ring and rose their hands to touch gloves. The young rookie was still obviously nervous but was moving her head from side to side, gloves up, shifting her body constantly to try avoiding getting hit before any strikes were thrown.

But to no avail. Era let out a sharp, crisp jab, which landed right on the rookies' face. Still a little stunned, she tried to continue her attempt at elusive movement. Era let out another crisp jab, then another, then another with a right cross as a follow. Each connecting on the young rookies face. She attempted a clumsy overhand, but Era easily slipped it, ducking and coming straight up with an uppercut. The bell rang and they both returned to their corner.

Cassius talked to the young rookie in the corner. Era tried listening, hearing a faint "You see, it ain' so bad. You can do some mo! Since you know you can handle dis', don' be so scared this time. Try throwin' some mo' combos, you got this!"

The bell rang again, and the two moved to the center of the ring again. The rookie seemed a little calmer this time. She started off with a double jab. Then another. Then a cross. Albeit impressed, Era effortlessly slipped each punch. Era could sense that the girl was quickly learning to use her fear as a foundation. Era let out another jab, but the rookie slipped it. Feeling generous and wanting to test her, she let out a slow double jab so the rookie could catch it. Slip, weave. The rookie was slowly overcoming her fear. Era shot a slow cross expecting the rookie to weave, but instead she slipped and threw a counter cross, popping Era right in the mouth.

Era felt a little drop of blood on her lip. She licked it off of her lips and gave a devious grin at the rookie. "Alright you little bastard.", she chuckled. She gave a quick power cross, connecting flat on the rookie's face, knocking her back a couple feet. After she landed, her knees slightly buckled, and Era came in for another power cross to knock her down. But before her cross connected, Cassius stopped her.

"Eeeeasy, girly." Cassius reprimanded. "You ain tryin' to kill her."

Era stopped, calmed herself and gave a quick apology. The two continued back and forth, slipping, jabbing, throwing some hooks and counters. Era, still taking it easy on the rookie wasn't afraid to put the pressure on to test her, but the rookie was learning with every passing second. A couple rounds later, Cassius ordered them both to stop.

The two stepped out, and after taking off her gloves, Era walked over to congratulate the rookie. But as she walked up, the rookie started puking into the nearby trash can. Cassius was behind her, talking while she was retching what little food she had in in her stomach and her shirt loose from the massive amount of sweat she had, Era decided she would congratulate her tomorrow, when she was more in control of herself and wasn't busy with Cassius.

Era walked to her gym bag, picked it up and turned around.

"See you later coach!" She yelled while waiving from across the floor.

Cassius smiled and waved back. Era smiled and headed to the shower.

It had been a while since Era sparred and she couldn't help but feel her body ache from sparring, even with a weaker opponent. Her biceps were tender, and her thighs were on fire. Her sports bra and hair were dripping with tidbits of sweat from the little sparring she did.

After a light shower, she changed over and headed home. Another short drive and she was back to her apartment. Another health-oriented meal, a light dessert, some stretching, and it was time to sleep.

Era sat on her bed leaned back onto her arms, causing her triceps to show and a thought crossed her mind. She felt as if she lost control over herself several times today. She yelled at Rusty, briefly went too hard on the rookie, and the young man crying reminded her of the way she used to be as a teenager. Her lack of control and previous childish mentality and being a crybaby. She hated it. And she hated herself for being like this. She let out a deep sigh and laid down.

## Part 2

## "Hellstorm devastation"

Era opened her eyes but immediately tried closing them again, feeling the pain of harsh winds and debris getting into her eyes. She squinted, tried to block the harsh winds by putting her hands and elbows up and turning away. A short time passed of a constant flurry of wind and tiny objects until she felt that familiar hand on her shoulder, and the wind immediately subsided. With the wind and debris gone, she felt comfortable enough to open her eyes and found herself in the eye of a hurricane with huge chunks of debris surrounding her. Wood, ripped clothes, car parts and unrecognizable scrap.

Era turned her head to look at the face of the hand on her shoulder and saw the Same smiling mask that she had been seeing for a while. Era let out a little grin wondering what this disaster would teach.

"What's up? What are we doing today?" Era giddily asked.

"Have patience." Said the Sage. He turned and faced the other side of the eye of the storm and stopped moving.

"Uhhh, can we go now? I don't wanna get hit by that fucking wind again."

"No." Stated the Sage.

"What the ...?" mumbled Era while making her what-the-fuck face. Era saw the eye of the wall approaching closer and closer. The sounds of the wind coming nearer and nearer. Roaring and ripping apart whatever object got in its way. Getting closer and closer until it was right in front of them.

"Brace yourself." Said the Sage. And Era once again began squinting her eyes and put her hands and elbows up to cover her face from the debris and wind. The raging gusts beating on her like a never-ending flurry of punches. She couldn't hear anything but the sounds of objects being torn apart and the blasts of powerful wind. Going on and on.

Era began thinking why the Sage was standing still rather than moving to another place. She had already felt the wind before she saw the Sage, so why go through it again? His lessons always appeared non-sensical at first, but he always had a point in the end. She would endure this like before.

The winds continued on and on for a substantial amount of time until finally subsiding. Era didn't realize it before, but her vision of the outlying region were blocked by the walls of the eye of the Hurricane. They were in a suburban area. Full of houses, trees, playgrounds, rec centers, schools, soccer mom vans, and daycares.

Or at least, what was left of these buildings.

The Sage looked down, as if he was disappointed. Era looked at him with a concerned face. "Is something wrong?" Era asked. The Sage looked up, turned around and faced her. And although he wore a mask that had an angry grin on it, she knew he was sad.

"Era, I am very disappointed in you. You know better than to lose your temper like that. You know better than to act so childishly."

Era's face dropped and she looked down. "…I know."

"What you see around you? All this destruction caused by this massive force of nature called a hurricane. This is the kind of destruction that you losing your temper will cause if you let it get out of control." The Sage admonished. "Be more aware of yourself, Era. You know better."

Era kept looking down and began to tear up in shame, but right before the tear made its way down her cheek, the

Sage placed his hand on her shoulder again. "It's ok, Era. I just expect more from you." That one tear slowly made its way down Era's cheek and landed on the Sage's black boots.

"Now dry your tears." He instructed. "We're barely getting started." Era quickly rubbed her cheeks and eyes with her hands and took a deep breath.

"Ok."

The Sage had already walked a few meters ahead of her while Era was drying her tears, so she had to run to catch up to him. After a quick jog she caught up to him. The two walked in silence until the terrain was suddenly transformed into a vast wasteland of smoldering ash. After looking around for a while the Sage asked her something. "What do you think this is?" Era continued to look around and saw what appeared to be dead leaves on the floor. She investigated further and saw charred remains of logs and a couple of burnt tree stumps. She then realized that they were in the dead embers of a forest. A huge forest.

"We're in a forest after a wildfire." Said Era as she knelt to pick up a burnt branch.

"Precisely." Said the Sage. "A raging wildfire that was so destructive that it consumed everything in this forest. Every tree, every animal, every piece of vegetation."

The Sage face Era. "And this is what hatred does, Era." She looked up at him, dropped the branch and stood up to face him. "All encompassing hatred will consume everything in your life. Anger is destructive, yes, But hatred will consume everything in your life when left unchecked."

Era glanced at how enormous the charred remains of the forest was again. "I guess hatred can consume pretty much anyone, huh?" Asked Era.

"Yes." Said the Sage. "If left unchecked. Now let's move on."

The Sage turned and started walking. Era took one last look at the dead embers of the forest. Once again taking in how big the fire must have been to totally consume such a large forest. She then turned and ran to catch up to the sage.

The two walked on and on until eventually reaching a cliff overlooking an ocean. A gentle breeze hit them both as they reached the edge of the cliff. The sun shone brightly overhead and some clouds off in the distance slowly moving towards the horizon. The scenery was one of peace and tranquility. But immediately broken by the sight before them.

A giant maelstrom. The size of a stadium and several large boats caught by its grip. Era could visibly see the sailors on the boat. Sobbing and crying. Screaming in the fetal position.

"DUDE! WE HAVE TO HELP THEM!!" Era yelled.

"Relax." Instructed the Sage. "They've already given in."

Era tilted her head in confusion and looked down at the

sailors again. As she looked more closely, she could see that the sailors were covering their ears while in the fetal positions, eyes tightly shut as tears ran down their snot covered face.

The boats circled around and around the maelstrom getting closer and closer into the eye. The sailors' screams grew louder and louder. And Era could see their hands gripping their ears tighter, and their eyes shutting tighter as well. The boats circled around and around the maelstrom until finally, it swallowed each one. One by one. Sinking to the bottom of the ocean.

"Sadness and despair are a lot like that maelstrom, Era." Explained the Sage. They suck you in and will bring you down to never be seen again. And a lot of people act like those sailors do. They block everything out during their sadness and despair. And then the maelstrom sucks them down into the depths."

Era looked down in pity to the sailors doomed to stay in the depths of the ocean. She raised her hand and started biting her fingernails. And she began diving into her memories.

"What's wrong?" Asked the Sage. "Are you remembering what it felt like to feel the crushing weight of the depths?"

And Era suddenly remembered all those times she had been alone in a room, hugging her knees, tears running down her snot covered face. Just like the sailors. She remembered crouching down, covering her ears, being left alone in depths of her despair. And her pupils dilated as she began remembering more details of the darkest times in her life. Being covered in mental chains, shackled by her own despair.

Era breaths became rapid as she began gripping her arms.

The memories continued. Being totally alone, with nothing When she had no one, and felt like she was being crushed by the deepest depths of the abyss that sucked her down and constantly kept her there, unable to breathe, or think, and constantly FELT LIKE SHE WAS SUFFOCATING, DYING, UNABLE TO BREATH AND LOSING CONTROL AND UNABLE TO MOVE WHILE EVERYTHIN AROUND HER WAS OUT OF CONTROL AND-

The Sage grabbed her shoulder. "Era. It's ok." He reassured.

After feeling his hands, Era slowed her breathing and released her grip on her arms. The Sage gave a warm feeling of power and reassurance. She took a deep breath and let out a big exhale, releasing her despair.

"Let's move on." Said the Sage.

They began walking again. Era continued trying to calm herself down from the memories. But the Sage placed his hand on her shoulder the second she began to regress.

The two walked towards what seemed to be a city. But not the same city they had visited when she saw things

from many perspectives. It was just another, run of the mill city. The two walked throughout the streets, passing restaurants, cars, high rise buildings, lamp posts, billboards, and many other things.

The reached a fountain that was in the middle of the entire city, where many streets seemed to intersect. They could both see rows of buildings and cars in every direction. The city was massive. Era wondered how much time it took to build such a city.

Suddenly, the ground began to tremble. Era immediately grabbed for the Sages arm. He grabbed her hand with his other arm to ensure she wouldn't fall. The streets began to crack, trees shaking so hard that the branches were being broken off. Small buildings began to collapse, roofs concaving into the 4 walls, then the walls themselves coming down. The billboards came crashing down, the pictures breaking and being left splintered all over the ground. Every stone piece of art being toppled from the force of the ground shaking. But the worst was yet to come.

The high-rise buildings began to buckle. Some began cracking higher up top, while some came undone at the base. Building's hundreds of feet tall and weighing thousands upon thousands of pounds came crashing down with unimaginable force. The concrete shattering all around, chunks of the building flying everywhere and crushing whatever was underneath it. The dust from broken concrete filled the city air.

By the time the ground stopped shaking, there wasn't a single building left standing. The streets were filled with debris of everything she had taken notice of before. Restaurants concaved in; billboards toppled with the images kissing the ground. Desks and chairs, pallets and lamps that were inside of the high-rise buildings all littered the ground. The sound of water from broken pipelines shooting up and car alarms echoed in the city.

Era stood there, shocked to her core, tightly grabbing on to the Sages arm. She couldn't bring herself to speak or move. All she could do is look at the absolute disaster that just took place.

The Sage took a deep breath and started explaining. "You see how shaking the foundation of things can cause so much destruction, Era? That's exactly how fear is. A deep rotting fear can shake a person to their very core and destroy everything that they've worked for." Era looked up at the Sage and release his arms. The two then moved to face each other, and he placed both of his hands on her shoulders.

The Sage continued, "We cannot let fear shake who we are, or we will lose everything that we work for." Era looked directly at the Sage and nodded her head.

He released her shoulders and turned around. "Come Era." He said.

The two began walking again, towards a destination unknown to Era. Working their way through the debris and destruction of the city, they eventually made their way out.

After taking some time to ponder everything that just happened, the Sage decided to reemphasize some things.

"Emotions are like these storms and natural disasters, Era." Said the Sage. Anger will destroy everything in its path just like that hurricane. Hatred will consume everything and leave nothing left if unchecked. Like that wildfire. Sadness will suck you in and never let you out if you allow it to. And fear is like those tremors of the earthquake, shaking everything and destroying everything that you have built." He lifted his hand and pointed in a direction behind Era. "However.", He continued.

Era looked in the direction that the Sage was pointing in and saw vast plains of grass. And hundreds of wind turbines covered these plains. Each one turning as the winds of the plains pushed every blade, causing a consistent rotation with each turbine tower.

"You are aware of what those are, correct?" Inquired the Sage.

"Uhm. Duh. They're turbines. They generate power from the wind." And as Era said this, something clicked in her thoughts. Hurricanes. Destruction. Unchecked emotions. Wind turbines. Powers. Control. She raised her hand to her mouth and started biting her nails, thinking.

"The unforgiving winds of a hurricane can cause destruction, but we can also harness power from wind. Too much uncontrolled anger can be destructive, but a controlled anger can be useful?" Era said.

"Good, Era." Said the Sage. "Let's move on."

The two once again started walking again. They walked on and on until coming across another forest, but this one untainted by the engulfing flames of a wildfire. They ventured inside the forest, full of vegetation and wildlife. They followed a trail of footprints that eventually led them to a village. And the village had the warmth of fire everywhere.

Several fires in clay stoves and cooking statues. Grills and kabobs everywhere. And the people of the village were all enjoying cooking the properly roasted meat that the fire made possible.

Era looked around more and more and saw something. A man in front of what seemed to be a large oven. He grabbed a large pair of tongs and opened the door. A gust of heat with scattered embers rushed out of the structure. He stuck his tongs inside and grabbed a red-hot piece of metal and extracted it. He then placed the red-hot metal on an anvil and began hammering away at it.

"So, these people all learned to utilize the fire to cook and also figured out blacksmithing.?", Asked Era.

"The same flames that engulfed the other forest and everything in it can be used for something good, Era." Said the Sage. "As you said, these people learned to use fire for cooking and blacksmithing. And it has many more uses."

The Sage continued. "In a similar manner, Maybe you can utilize hatred to hate your own weakness and make them your strength. Burn away the things about yourself that you dislike with the flames of hatred. Maybe you can hate the negative things of the world and work to make things better. Sometimes, we can use hatred for good."

The concept the Sage was explaining to Era seemed extremely foreign to her. 'Using hatred for good?' All that kept popping into her head were the teachings that the priests and pastors would all try to beat into her young mind way back when.

"Those with a hateful heart can never reach the eternal kingdom of the gods!!"

"Hate will only stir up strife and cause problems for the one engaging in such a heinous emotion!"

"You cannot hate someone and expect to love the gods! The gods are love and will not accept hatred!"

"Love everyone, never have hate in your heart!"

But while these old relics of her past were screaming in her head, she would also remember how these same priests and pastors would steal from offerings and would get arrested for possession of heroin and drunk driving. Maybe these old words weren't true and everything the Sage was saying was making more sense.

"Ok.", said Era. "Where to now?"

The Sage turned around and began walking. Era took a quick glance at the village that just learned to harness the power of fire. Hoping she could do what they have done, she turned around and caught up with the Sage.

They continued on for some time until they came to another cliff. But rather than the ocean, this cliff overlooked a huge lake with a grey colored dam. "What is that?" The sage asked while pointing.

"It's a dam. Duh." Scoffed Era.

"Not just a dam. A hydroelectric dam." The Sage pointed down to a building, as if to ask Era what it was.

"Oh! That's a powerhouse! It houses the generators." Said Era.

"You're doing good in school, Era." Congratulated the Sage. "At this point I don't think I need to tell you the analogy."

Era looked at the Sage. "The same element. Water. That swallowed those boats and the crews. Can be used for power."

The Sage was listening intently, motioning his hand in circles with his pointer finger out to signal to her to keep going.

Era continued, "And that dam was built and has a solid foundation of earth. And while it is true that earth can move from earthquakes and destroy foundations, you can also build on earth to MAKE solid foundations. Just like the way the Dam is built on the mountains that are holding it."

The Sage faced her again. "Perfect.", he said.

"All these elements can also be harnessed and used, Era. That hurricane's powerful wind destroyed everything in its path. But those wind turbines use wind to generate power. The fire can be destructive, but sometimes a little destruction can promote life. The water can also produce power as well. Those foundations are made from Earth and can stand for long periods of time. Again, the elements are like our emotions. A rush of anger can give you power and focus. Hating the right things can make you love life that much more. Sadness can be used to make art. And fearing the right things can give you a good foundation for life. Negative emotions can help us and are just as important as positive emotions."

Era looked down and began biting her nails again and started getting lost in thought. After thinking for a short period of time she stopped and looked up.

"Was that shadow I first fought with my negative emotions? Was embracing that shadow the first step in learning to use all these negative emotions?" Asked Era.

Era felt the Sage smile behind his face covered mask. All the pieces were starting to connect and everything the Sage was trying to show her started fitting in with what seemed to be one grand narrative. After Eras mind had slowed down, the Sage answered.

"Yes."

# Chapter 5

## "Theory of Infinite Beauty"

Era woke to a noisy alarm clock. The kind of alarm that made you want to throw it against the wall and shatter it to a million pieces. But rather than lose control over her emotions, she would simply press the 'off' button and leave it at that. This made her feel a bit better about last week's emotional outbursts.

She sat up, wiped the drool from the corners of her mouth and looked at her calendar. It was Saturday. No school, no work, and no training, and was happy to sleep in, well into the midday. A day to choose to do whatever she wanted. She uncovered her lower body from the blanket, placed her feet on the floor, stood and started stretching.

"Start every day by gettin' yo' blood and thoughts flowin', girly!" Cassius advice to Era was something she truly took to heart.

But not perfectly. She thew herself back on to her bed and let out a long deep yawn. Extending her arms over her head and legs splayed out to totally stretch all of her limbs, She let out another little squeak before she stopped and laid there for another couple of minutes.

"Alright for realsies, I got to get up now." Era thought to herself. She stood back up and after getting her yawns out once more, she began some dynamic stretches to loosen up her tight defined muscles and get her blood flowing. After 5 minutes of moving around and waking up more, she quickly put on a sports bra to keep her boobs from flailing everywhere while she did her exercises. She grabbed the 70 lb curl bar by her wall and started curling away. Then on to some pushups, squats, then sit-ups. She continued the circuit several times, just enough to get a bit of a pump; her biceps slightly popping out and sweat slowly running down her cheeks. Now she was fully awake.

As soon as she was finished, she did her usual morning routine. A long shower, hot as the fiery pits of a Satan dwelling hell. After finishing and drying off, she immediately heard the stomach under her tight abs growl for nourishment. "Right… ooon schedule." Era thought. She walked to the kitchen area of the studio and brought out the foods to make her typical breakfast. Eggs, lean ham, and whole wheat toast.

"I'm surprised I haven't gotten sick of eating the same bullshit every day." Era thought to herself. But she also knew a stable and consistent routine was one of the keys to keep her dark thoughts at bay and be successful in all of her efforts.

After finishing and washing her dishes, she decided to spend the day studying. Finals for her first semester of college were just around the corner, after all. She put on her typical school attire. A snug black crop t shirt, jeans, and her boots. She gathered all her notes, stuffed them into her backpack and headed to campus, since she wasn't able to study in her cramped little studio. The temptation to sleep would be too much.

A quick walk outside, a short drive, and another walk later she was right outside of her usual study spot. As she was about to open the entrance door, she felt a hand on her shoulder.

"BOO!!" The owner of the hand yelled.

"AAHH!!" Squealed Era as she jumped and quickly turned around.

An adorable chuckling grin towered over her head. She couldn't quite make out the face because the sun was shining directly into her dark green eyes, but the voice sounded familiar. After shifting a bit, she saw the face clearly.

"What's up, Era?" Said Arrow. "Came to study?"

Era was still a little flustered from being scared but was able to gather her words to give an awkward response. "Uhhh.. yeah." She said while giving an uneven grin.

Arrow opened the door to let her in. "Me too. Finals are coming up, so I need a bit of extra studying."

They both walked inside the building, looking for a spot but saw only one table open. All of the tables were full of study groups.

"Yooouuu… don't mind sharing a table, do you?" Asked Arrow.

"No, not really." Era replied.

The two pulled seats out with one seat in between them. Era felt somewhat of a tension since this was her first time seeing him outside of the bar and class. He maintained the same level of chipper charm that he had at work. She assumed it was a mask that he put on to get better tips.

Arrow opened his backpack and pulled out one monstrous book that read "Introduction to quantum mechanics" and a thinner book that said, "dummies guide to literature". He opened up the larger book, took out his binder and started his studying. Era did the same.

A few arduous hours of scribbled words, equations, problems, reading, and several headaches later, they both decided to take a break. Arrow put his hands behind his head and leaned back on his chair while exhaling loudly, clearly feeling mentally wore out. Era put her elbows on the table and rubbed her face with both of her hands to soothe her tired brain.

"BLEGH. College, AmIrite?" Laughed Arrow while still leaning back.

"Heh. Yeah." Answered Era. She still wasn't quite sure how to interact with Arrow. She skittishly fiddled with her hands while looking down at the table.

"You're still boxing right? Been up to anything else?" He asked.

Era still wasn't sure if he was hoping for more tips when she went back to the bar, or if it was genuine interest.

"Uuhhh yeah. But no, not really doing anything else. Just work, to be honest." Answered Era. Still not sure how to interact, she hugged her elbows, leaned forward, and let out a small grin directed at him.

There was a brief stale silence, and a vibe of tension was still in effect. Both stayed in their respective poses for a while until Era decided to try and break it.

"What about you? Have you been up to anything else? Decide on a major yet?" Asked Era.

"Actually, yes! I went through with it and went with physics." He stopped leaning back and put his hands on the table. "I've been getting really into it, and I'm loving the classes. The concepts, astronomy, stars. It actually gets hella tripped out when you start getting deep into the concepts. A lot of the best scientists were also philosophers. Did you know that?"

The mention of philosophy peaked Era's interest in the conversation. Her classes and the lessons the Sage was teaching her suddenly became relevant in a real conversation.

"I didn't know that!" Era said. "Psychology and philosophy cross sometimes, too. That's really cool!"

Arrow continued. "By the way, I actually have been doing something else. Do you know what spoken word is?"

"Not a fucking clue." Said Era, raising her eyebrow.

"It's basically like a poetry meeting for people to come

in and share their poetry or speeches. I've really been getting into those lately." Said Arrow. He suddenly had a tone in his voice that faintly resembled embarrassment.

"Oh, wow. I didn't really think you were into poetry and stuff?" Said Era while holding her cheeks in a playful shock.

"Well, I didn't think someone as pretty and awkward as you would be a boxer if it wasn't for your physique." Teased Arrow.

Era laughed and rested her cheeks on one of her hands. "Well, have you shared any of your stuff yet? Where do these things usual happen?"

"Well, I haven't shared any yet. I'm actually working on one right now. It gets kind of gut wrenching standing in front of all those people. You're basically on a stage, giving a performance." Era realized the faint tone of embarrassment was essentially Arrow having stage fright.

"I know how that feels. I used to compete, remember?" Said Era.

"Remind me to never make you mad." Said Arrow while smiling and holding his hands out to block any potential punches.

Era let out a faint laugh, still resting her cheek on her hand. "You could practice with me if you'd like. It'll help you for when you actually do it."

"Oh, dude, that would be great. Can we try right now?"

Asked Arrow.

"Sure." Era answered.

Arrow took in a long, deep breath and began.

"Right, so I'm reading a book on string theory. It's been a while since I've actually read it because of finals, but I know where I'm at. This book is fascinating to me because it tries to explain what everything is fundamentally composed of. Not matter, but vibrating strings of energy. Essentially atoms to atoms. I haven't finished so this is an incomplete thought, but several things that have stuck out to me."

Era noticed his tone of voice had changed. From sweet and charming to passionate and serious. As he began what would be an epic rambling, she became honed in on his words.

"Ok." Said Era. She motioned her hands, encouraging him to continue.

"One thing in particular that stuck out to me is everything is nothing but chance, and anything is possible. The laws of physics still apply.

Era briefly interrupted "Like Newtons laws, chemical interactions, and all that?"

Arrow answered. "Exactly! And everything generally follows a certain pattern. If you combine the two ideas it could be thought of like this; if you know two elements react with each other because you're good at chemistry, the chance of them reacting is 99.99999999999999%. But because there is a slight chance that they will sit there as if nothing happened. But this is like a

0.00000000000000000000001% chance. Does that make sense?"

"I'm actually taking a chemistry class, so this makes a lot of sense." Said Era.

"So that being said, I try to think about this in relation to parallel universes. It has been highly speculated that there are other universes."

Era immediately started remembering her philosophy classes and became increasingly more interested in Arrows words. She grasped her hands together in front of her lips, now invested and focusing on Arrows spoken word practice.

He continued "But what if these universes were also composed of these vibrating strings? On top of that, considering what I've read the universe should not really exist. It should be failing, collapsing within itself, not stable at all. Even newtons laws, which have been the basis for pretty much all of modern physics, has been under assault. Some theories have been disproven."

"Like what?" Asked Era, squinting her eyes, focusing on the interaction.

"Like the cosmological principle." Answered Arrow. "In one of my classes, we had a researcher come in and tell us they think they may have discovered an object that has WAY more mass than considered possible in the universe. Things are basically supposed to be pretty uniform across the universe, but this thing breaks that theory. And so many things are left unexplained and are huge mysteries in the universe."

Era noticed his words becoming a bit more rapid, and even more passionate. Like he was coming up to some grand point.

"So, I thought, well according to string theory anything is possible right? What if these other "universes" are also composed of these strings. So, it's possible that there are infinitely many parallel universes but none of them ever came to actually be. But one did. Ours. It could have been trillions, quadrillions of years or even an eternity past until finally there was sufficient chance for the universe that we live in to come to be."

Era was totally homed in on Arrow's words at this point.

"This is purely speculation, but we could be one in the infinite number of universes to ever sprout into existence. And we live in one of billions of galaxies. In a teeny tiny piece of that galaxy. On a rock that is one of the smaller portions of an ordinary solar system in a section of the galaxy that is actually able to sustain life. In a tiny section of time out of millions of years that life has been on this earth.

Arrow turned to face Era.

"And you. In the midst of all this chaos, was sprouted out of millions of cells competing as the result of two people meeting in the billions of people to ever live on this planet. The chances of you existing are inconceivable, it doesn't make sense on a quantum or mathematical level. And yet here you are, reading this, living life and fighting the impossible odds that you have been given not only by science, but by the life you have lived."

Era had her hands on her cheeks at this point, flushing a light red.

"This goes so much further than saying "You're one in a million." I'm not saying one in a billion. Or even a trillion. This is saying you are one in an infinity. Do you think you're not important? Do you think you don't matter? I think otherwise. I think you are the result of something sprouting out of an impossible chance. You are infinitely beautiful."

Finishing his one-man performance, Arrow let out a small sigh. "I call that little speech my 'Theory of infinite beauty'".

Era remained motionless for a couple of seconds before taking a deep breath.

"I loved it." She calmly said. "I absolutely loved it."

"Any constructive criticism?" Arrow asked.

"The only thing I can think of is wondering if whoever is listening will understand the concepts you're talking about. If they don't, the bigger message may be lost on them if they don't. Plus, I'm not sure if the audience will actually interact with you like I did." Replied Era.

"Good point." Said Arrow. "I should probably work on it more."

Era looked outside and noticed the Sun had started going down. Most of the students had vacated the room a while ago and the only ones left were packing up their stuff.

"I'm tired of studying. I'll probably be heading out now." Said Arrow while standing up, stretching, and letting out little exhales of exhaustion.

"Yeah, me too." Said Era. "Where did you Park?"

"Not too far." Said Arrow. He had began gathering his notes, putting away his writing gear, and shoving his comically sized textbook in his backpack. "Wanna walk together?"

Era smiled and nodded. She began packing her things as well. By the time she had finished, Arrow was waiting at the exit, holding the door open.

The two took off and held a consistent conversation the entire time. Era told her about Rusty and the kids in her class. Arrow told her about the other bartender he worked with who was also his boss. His name is Pepe and he's always grumpy because of how Arrow is always late because he tends to lose track of time. He also brought up his older sister Hedone and how he was raised. Era told him about Cassius and more of her boxing training, and Arrow told her how he had been writing poetry for a long time and was excited to actually start sharing it with people.

20 minutes of conversation in, and Era had realized a few things. She was no longer unsure on how to interact with Arrow. Most if not all of the awkwardness had dissipated, and she spoke to him with confidence. After sharing his poetry, any and all ice had been shattered and interacting with him came very naturally. She also realized that he wasn't trying to interact with her for better tips, it was a genuine approach. And lastly, she realized how short the time she spent with him felt. They were already near their vehicles.

"Ok, well. I'll be here tomorrow to study again. The Bar is closed on Sunday. Will you be here?" Asked Arrow, while fidgeting his hands and hoping for a positive answer.

Era gave a soft grin. "Definitely."

# Chapter 6

## Part 1

Several years had gone by, and Era had been taking notes and was learning from everywhere. Every person she met, and everything she participated in. Every class, every training session, every child that she mentored, she learned something.

After her first semester she had taken a theology class on religions of the past. Groups of people that wore extravagant feathered headdresses that would sacrifice people to their gods. Other groups of people in the freezing tundra's that believed in powerful gods that would one day destroy the world in an epic clash.

She wondered what circumstances of their culture caused them to sacrifice people and believe the things they believed. Was it their environments? Possibly misconceptions? These questions lingered in the back of her head for a significant period of time.

The next semester she had also taken a modern-day religion class where the professors briefly explained some of the popular religion in the current societies of various countries.

Several religions caught her eye and made her wanted to dig in further, One religion stressed a few key aspects.

Such as the Vades; the holy texts that had the supreme authority in that religion. The religions also stressed the concept of the soul as an immortal being inside every person that is to be reincarnated in a perpetual cycle of life and death until that being can attain Darma, the perfect reality where the being can become one with the ultimate being and be free from the cycle of life and death. And that ultimate being is everything that exists.

These concepts were what Era remembered from those particular classes and did her best to understand them. Another religion simultaneously disgusted and intrigued her. The religion that she cast aside due to her upbringing. A religion that stressed the belief in Jevoh as the supreme being, that punished humanity for their choices, Every person is evil and imperfect and only through the self-sacrifice of this supreme being can people be freed from eternal damnation and suffering after death and achieve salvation. And this same religion caused many wars through the teachings of raging war to fulfill certain prophesies.

Era had very distinct memories of those practicing this religion screaming in her face on how she will being damned for eternity for not saying certain things and acting a certain way.

"YOU'LL BE IN INFERNO FOREVER!!"

"A PAINFUL FATE AWAITS YOU IF YOU KEEP ACTING LIKE THIS!!"

"STOP THINKING THAT OR YOU WILL BE IN

ETERNAL PAIN."

The class reminded her of these horrible words, but also stressed the importance of unconditional love and kindness.

Another class stressed the teachings of the legendary enlightened one, some through the holy books called the Triptaka, which had 3 in depth lovely sections. 1 taught everything is perpetually changing, temporary things will suffer, and all life involves pain. The enlightened one also helped others through his teachings of the 4 honorable truths and the righteous 8-fold path may one be free of the pain of life. The 4 truths that were the reality of suffering, what causes it, the end of it, and the final road. The righteous 8-fold path that explained you must follow the correct view, resolve, speech, conduct, livelihood, efforts, mindfulness, and self-concentration. And through following these teachings, you can become free from the suffering and ignorance of the world. A religion that taught that although we are all separate, all is one.

This religion caught Era's attention because it stressed focus, meditation, and to become free. Just as she has been desiring all her life. The focus also made her think of her boxing training; total focus and awareness of what she is doing during her matches.

Era did notice that many of these religions had striking similarities. Many of these religions caused war and strife though their conflicting beliefs, but also stressed love, sacrifice, and kindness, and becoming something greater. So different, yet so many similarities.

Era also kept the same job as a teachers aid during these years. Rusty stayed at the same school, so they would still interact with each other. As Rusty grew older, he became bigger, and his behavior became more erratic. And most of all, he was becoming more angry and Era noticed the effects of his home life.

"Hey, Rusty!" She would say.

"Oh… Hey, Miss Era." Was his typical response.

"You want to talk? I notice you're still keeping to yourself during recess and drawing."

"I'm ok, Miss Era. But thank you." He would respond.

Era attempted to mentor him and help him throughout the years, but more often than not, Rusty would close her out. But he knew that Era cared about him.

Aside from Rusty, Era would mentor every youngling that came through Miss Magist's class. Timid kids that needed some encouragement to bring them out of their shell, some kids that needed extra instruction, some that needed a hug, and some that needed a scolding. Whatever kids came through the classes Era and Miss Magist would do their best to teach them and help them grow.

On the days she didn't have work, Era would usually head to HallaVal for some training with coach Cassius. She had been improving more and more and even won a few amateur tournaments and events, causing coach Cassius to encourage her more and more to start sign up for pro tournaments, but Era remained undecided as she continued with work and college.

And during these years Era continuously would catch Arrow in between classes. They became consistent study partners and would chit chat and share things during their study sessions. Era would tell Arrow about her efforts with her training and Arrow would tell her about his spoken word events.

These conversations would often lead to Arrow getting into long rants about his classes and how he would incorporate them into his performance pieces. And the two had become close enough to not let politeness get in the way of their conversations.

"Ok, but do you know the concept of the big bang… ERA?!"

"Ok, first of all, stop yelling at me." Said Era while holding her hand up with her pointer finger up, swerving her head. "Second of all, no. The actual fuck is that?"

"So basically, before the universe was what it is now, everything was in a small single insanely dense point. Everything was one." Arrow said. He was smiling ear to ear, and his voice was bleeding with excitement.

"What? That doesn't make any sense." Laughed Era.

"Well, it doesn't to you, but it's a crazy concept for me. And there's another theory where eventually, the entire universe will regress back into the single point. So, everything will become one again in billions and billions of years. Crazy to think about, huh?" Arrow said, leaning back into his chair.

"Kind of like the birth and death of the universe?"
Asked Era.

"Wasn't thinking of it like that, but yeah that works!"
Answered Arrow. "This theory is called the big crunch."
We went over it in one my astronomy classes last week.
There's a lot more to it but I don't want to bore you. Haha."

"You're not boring me; I like learning about all this
stuff." Said Era. "I just don't understand it as much as you
do."

"The wildest part about all of this is, it's just the
beginning. Science in general is missing so many pieces
that it's a continuous process. Some things are basically
factual, but a lot of it is purely speculation based on what
we know, you know?"

"Ok, so like. If I punch you in the face, you'll definitely
have a broken nose. But who knows if you'll actually
forgive me?" Era joked and she clenched her fists and put
them against Arrow's face.

"Whoaa hooo hoooo!!" Arrow exclaimed while raising
his hands in submissions. "Yes, like that! But no need to be
hostile!"

Their interactions would continue in this same fashion
throughout the next few semesters. Sometimes after study
sessions, and sometimes at the Elysium bar. Every time Era
would come in during Arrows shift, he was always late.
And him and his partner would have the exact same

dialogue.

"Sorry, I'm late man." Arrow would say.

"Yer always late ya fuckin idiot." Pepe would answer.

And the ever so consistent answer, "Yeah man, school it brutal." He an odd tick of running his hand through his curly dark brown hair as he said this. Arrow would serve patrons, clean glasses, and the two would banter whenever they had the chance.

One particular concept from her classes that Era would bring up was from her psychology classes that her Professor Carl would teach. A concept called 'the unconscious'. As Era understood it, it was essentially a blank slate of types of people that humanity could be. And everyone was connected to each other through the collective unconscious. All that people were and did was built on top of the ocean that is the unconscious.

Another class she took note of was from another of her philosophy class that Professor Fredrich taught. A class that spoke of the goal of humanity. Rather than being consumed with the meaning and the concepts of right and wrong, one should seek the truth beyond all of that. In becoming greater and having a will to become stronger, one could ascertain true freedom.

In one of her classes, one of her assignments was to read a book called "So says Zoroaster". A book that told the story of a wise man that spent years in the mountains to observe humanity and became wise through his observations. But when he came down in attempt to help humanity, no one understood his teachings. So, the wise man went back into reclusion and began waiting for the higher beings that would happily embrace his teachings.

The book, coupled with the class teachings took a very permanent spot in Era's memories. One that lasted for several semesters.

Era went about every single day of the years noticing people, connecting things that they do. The way all of their various religions are all similar, and those similar concepts being shown in psychology and philosophy. The things that she and Arrow would talk about, along with the way she and Miss Magist would work together found their way into these thoughts as well. She knew she didn't have the immaculate understanding as she should have, but she understood them in her own way.

Yet throughout all these years, Era had a lingering loneliness in the back of her mind. Though she had been learning and growing, improving, and making friends in Arrow and Miss Magist, mentoring younglings, and growing as an athlete, she hadn't seen the Sage the entire time.

No new lessons to be learned from him, no new landscapes, no new perspectives. She missed being with him and every time she woke up without seeing him, it took its toll on her heart. Every night she would go to sleep, with a hope lingering in the back of her mind.

And for the first time in years, her hope would be rewarded.

# Part 2

# "Enlightenment lies in the nexus"

Era opened her eyes and found herself standing on a low-rise cliff, overlooking a vast unending landscape of plains. She took a few steps forward to see what the cliff was above and saw a web of winding, crossing roads all across these plains. She turned around and saw the Sage, and what appeared to be the beginning to these roads.

"Hello, Era." The Sage happily greeted while raising one of his hands. Era felt his unseen smile behind his mask as he spoke.

The Sage had a certain level of glee in `his voice. A little less serious and noticeably more excited than usual. She ran up to give him a hug. As their bodies met, his arms wrapped around hers and they held each other tightly.

"I haven't seen you in FOREVER!! Where have you been!? I've missed youuu!" Whined Era while hopping up and down.

The Sage smiled behind his mask and replied, "I missed you too. I'm sorry, but I've been busy making these roads. It was taking a while, and I wasn't able to see you until I was finished."

Era took a step back and began pouting, crossing her arms and gave the ground a little stomp.

"But I am here now." Reassured the Sage. "And I am quite excited to show you what I've been building for the past couple of years."

The Sage put his hands on Era's shoulders just like he used to. It was so comforting to Era.

"Are you ready to begin?" Asked the Sage.

Era gave a devious smirk and answered. "Duh."

The two took their first steps on the beginning of the path and began walking. Excited as ever to learn as she used to, Era all but began running as they started down the path.

"So, if you built these paths, does that mean you built the cities and those gardens too?" Asked Era.

The Sage chuckled. "No. I told you when showing you the city where I showed you different perspectives, it was my first time seeing that city as well."

Era gave her what-the-actual-fuck look and shook her head. "Then what about the garden? Or the science buildings?"

"Those were already there when I met you there, Era." Answered the Sage. "For now, let's just focus on what is in front of us."

Era, confused at his words as always, complied, and looked forward.

"So, you saw all those different paths, right?" Asked the Sage. "What did you notice about them?"

"Weeellll… I noticed a lot of them looked different. Some were finished, some weren't. Some had signs, some didn't, and they were mostly all different colors. That's about it."

"Not bad, but you are missing something important." Said the Sage. "There are quite a few different paths that we will be taking, but we'll take this one first."

The two arrived at the beginning of one of the paths. Era raised her eyes and saw that it was filled with blood and bodies. This entire path was colored differently from the others because the sun was making the pavement shimmer with a spectacular red color. And the small patches of black were decaying bodies left to rot.

Era got angry and turned to face the Sage to throw a cross, but he slipped and easily avoided it. "WHAT THE HELL. YOU MADE THIS PATH AND DECORATED IT WITH BODIES AND BLOOD YOU FUCKING ASSHOLE!!!???"

The Sage stood still and took a deep breath. "I said I built the path; I didn't say that others didn't take it after I built it."

Era took a step back. "What… what path is this then?"

"This." Said the Sage. "Is one of the bloody paths of religion."

After the Sage said this, Era looked around, paying more attention to more than just the decaying bodies and blood. She saw signs and banners that resembled crosses, half-moons, and wheels. Bodies burned with the word's 'heretic' and 'infidel'. Many of these bodies had armor, some seemed to be in tattered clothing. Some women, some men. Some women wearing revealing clothing, some women holding tightly to their babies who were also rotting. Some men cowering in their tattered clothing, and others sword in hand, dead in their pierced armor.

"Come on, Era." Said the Sage. Let's keep going down this path.

The two continued, stepping in a bloody puddle with every other step. "The path of religion often leads to these types of things, Era." Explained the Sage. And as he spoke, Era noticed various documents laying about the path. Holy books, scrolls of doctrines, letters, bribes, and mistranslated texts.

He continued, "And some people will cling so tightly to these things that they will unapologetically follow them and harm others because they think it is right."

Era looked around and saw more bodies and pools of blood. "But." Said the Sage. "Sometimes you'll see some peaceful moments on this path." He pointed up to a building on the side of the path and saw people on the outside, sitting around a fire peacefully, and singing.

"This is the path that many choose to take, Era. And it often ends in bloodshed, as a result of dogmatic doctrine made by zealots, but can also provide peace and happiness to people."

Era began to tear up, but before a single tear could run

down her cheek, the Sage placed his hands on her shoulder. "Let's go to the next path."

They turned around to begin another path that was right next to them. They both took a step forward and began another small journey. The pavement on this path was much sturdier and cleaner than the previous path. It was also more pleasant to look at compared to the bloody path of religion and every step felt secure.

But every so often, Era would notice a massive pothole or missing guardrails. Some of the signs every few hundred feet read something that didn't make sense. And some signs read something that made perfect sense, but another sign that contradicted it came immediately afterwards.

Every so often she would see billboards of old professors, men and women, arguing. Some shaking hands, and some were teaching classes.

"What path is this?" Asked Era.

"This is the incomplete path of Science." Said the Sage. "It's sturdy, and promising. But missing a lot of material, and sometimes, the design requires some retrofitting and maintenance. Who knows how long it will take until it's complete?

Era looked forward and saw the path had no end, it just stopped in the middle of what seemed to be a construction site, still incomplete and being worked on.

"I'm assuming we're stopping here." Said Era. She turned to look, and the Sage was already walking back, presumably to the next path.

The Sage turned his head to glance at Era. "Duh."

The two continued for hours on various paths. Some of the most noticeable were the paths of philosophy. It was full of signs that made no sense, and graffiti all over the smaller ones. Some signs had nothing at all, and others had nothing more than a single word written on it.

Another was the path of psychology. It had as many signs as the paths of religion and felt as stable as the path of science, but she noticed the sings were constantly changing being changed and painted over with something new.

They continued on other paths of religion. Some just as bloody at the first, with banners of a crescent moon on them, One had a giant billboard with a meditating human silhouette at the end of it. Many different symbols were on various banners.

Some of the science paths were complete and done, flawless and perfect. While others barely even had a beginning. One of the paths of psychology had man covers that seemed ready to burst, clearly repressed pressure underneath, while another went over a vast ocean that had human shadows of different archetypes below it. Some looked like an animal possessed woman, one a pregnant woman, and one looked like an old man. They traveled paths on paths for hours and hours.

"Have you noticed yet, Era?" Asked the Sage.

"Noticed what?" She responded.

"These paths keep crossing each other. Some cross here and there, some are constantly crossing." Explained the Sage.

"Era raised her hand to grab her chin and bit her lip. "Sooooo… does that mean they all eventually cross at one point?" Asked Era.

The Sage gave an unseen smirk behind his mask.

"Let's keep walking." He said.

Finally, they reached the center. The nexus of every path they had taken. Every path of religions, peaceful or bloody, every path of science, philosophy, psychology, every mode of thought that made every single one of these paths. All crossed at this one point. Era looked around at the hundreds of paths and tried making sense of it all. She opened her mouth to speak, but the Sage spoke before she could.

"Every path comes from the same place, Era." Said the Sage. "And every perception is just a broken shard of what was once the whole truth."

And there, in the crossroads of all these roads. The bloody roads, the broken roads, the incomplete roads, the infinite, finite, ever changing number of roads that were thought; stood Era and the Sage. And as they both looked around to gaze at the various and endless roads, Era slowly reached for the Sages hand. He reached back and they tightly held hands, standing there together.

# Chapter 7

## Part 1

This day started with no birds chirping, and a cloudy sky that prevented any sunlight from breaking through Era's window to hit her sun kissed skin. Just a cold temperature from the shadows that the clouds cast. She noticed her alarm didn't go off, and only woke up out of sheer routine. Her clock must have faulted.

Era looked at the calendar on her wall and saw that she had no classes. Just Era's part time job as a teachers aid with Miss Magist. Rather than begin her usual routine of exercising and going to school, she took a light stretching routine to wake up, showered, had her usual meal, and headed to the primary school for some extra hours.

This was Era's 3rd year working with Miss Magist as a teacher's aide. During this particular year, one student caught her eye the same way Rusty did. But this child, was significantly worse off. Tattered clothes, an utterly defeated look in her eye, and whenever Era would ask her how she was doing while reaching her arms out to her, the young girl would immediately run into her arms and begin to tear up. Her desk marker read 'Ranyo'.

Every single time Era would talk with her, she would try to tell her positive things.

"It's ok to cry."

"Whatever is wrong, you can tell me."

"There's nothing wrong with you, baby girl."

"Life can be good."

These little lectures gave life to the little girl, the same way that Era's words would help Rusty.

This same little girl would devour the school's food to the point where Era wasn't sure if she actually chewed or not. Era would offer her snacks as well, which the young girl would scarf down in an instant.

Era had an inkling to check the little girl's body for marks, cuts, and bruises, under her clothes, but the schools and government policies prevented her from doing so. Era's suspicions grew as time passed.

And today was the day her suspicions would be confirmed.

During a math lecture that Miss Magist was giving the class, the classroom door opened with a loud slam. Before she could turn to see who opened it, she heard an extremely angry and concerned voice.

"Excuse me, ma'am?" Era turned to meet this deep voice, booming with authority. It was a peace officer, with a woman behind him. The woman had a badge that read 'child shielding agency' on her polo shirt.

"Is this child in this classroom?" The peace officer

asked while holding up a picture of a tattered and starved little girl. The house she was in was disgusting, with mouse holes and moth balls everywhere. Dirty dishes, but no refrigerator. And empty bottles of whiskey on the counter.

Era looked at the picture and upon closer inspection saw that it was Ranyo. The same little girl that she had been talking to and teaching alongside Rusty.

Miss Magist immediately and without hesitation walked up to the peace officer and agent.

"Yes. She is right here." Miss Magist pointed towards Ranyo as she began walking towards her, wrapped her arms around her and slowly picked her up to guide her to the two authorities.

The child shielding agent dropped to one of her knees and reached her hand out. "It's ok, Ranyo. Everything is ok now."

Ranyo reluctantly walked forward as Miss Magist slowly guided her forward with her hands on her back.

Miss Magist consoled Ranyo. "It's ok, honey bun. These nice people are going to take you away to a better place."

And as Miss Magist finished her consolation, Ranyo burst into tears and ran in to the Agents arms. The entire class was looking at the spectacle, not knowing what to do. Neither did Era.

The agents eventually led Ranyo out of the class, and a

short while later, the bell rang. Dismissing the children from their class.

Era waited until all the kids were gone and approached Miss Magist.

"Uhhh… What… what was that?" Era asked.

Miss Magist took a break from organizing her graded papers and lesson plans titled 'fun plans for the kids' and took a deep breath.

"I know an abused child when I see one, Era. I've been teaching for almost 15 years. And I know you saw it as well. Ranyo has been beat, starved, and all around treated horribly by her mother. And I know it's her mother because she's the only one on Ranyo's paperwork. She comes in every day with the same clothes, hungry as a rabbit. And I recently started noticing tiny spots of blood seeping through her clothes. Probably from cuts, maybe scratches."

Era's eyes dilated as Miss Magist spoke and she took a small step back.

Miss Magist continued. "I've been doing this for a while, Era. And I know that sometimes the best thing for a child is to get them away from their household. We may not see her again, but that's what's for the best. Anything to get Ranyo away from that monster that calls herself her mother.

Era stood there, in bewilderment.

Miss Magist continued to talk but her words began to

fade as Era unwillingly dove into her memories. An unknown parent beating her relentlessly, an old gross priest reaching out to her 10-year-old thighs, a missed meal for a misspoken word, nothing to wear as the adults laughed and drank the bad juice, belt marks, and bruises on her eyebrows from a clenched fist, thrown bottles, screaming, insults, broken walls, and -

"Era!!" Screamed Miss Magist as she shook Era by her shoulders. "Era!! What's wrong!!??"

Era's pupils adjusted and she came back to reality.

"OH! Sorry!" She said while smiling and awkwardly shaking her head. "Just spaced out for a second."

"Era… you started hyperventilating and your pupils were the size of a quarter. Are you ok?"

Era composed herself and took a deep breath. "Yes, Miss Magist."

She felt a knot form in her stomach, A familiar and ugly feeling. "Sorry, But I need to go now.", She said as she grabbed her bag and quickly scurried out of the classroom. Miss Magist stood there with a concerned look on her face as Era walked away.

As Era rushed to her car, she saw Rusty walking towards one of the exits of the schoolgrounds. She frantically walked towards him, grabbed him by his shoulder and spun him around.

She took a quick frantic breath while Rusty stood there

in shock.

"Rusty…" She started. "If there is anything wrong, come talk to me, ok??? Don't ever be afraid to come talk to me when something is wrong! If something is hurting you, let me know and we can work through it together, do you understand me??"

Rusty stood there with a panicked and confused look on his face and slowly shook his head. "Yes… Miss Era…" He stuttered.

Era stood up, mildly embarrassed from her dramatic interaction with a young boy that she wished someone had given to her when she was a kid. She swept the dust from her clothes, composed herself and gave Rusty a quick hug.

"See you later, Rusty." She said before walking away. Rusty continued his walk home after seeing Era walk away. Baffled, but blushing.

After entering her car, Era sat there in silence until the entire primary school was empty. All the kids were either picked up by their parents, took the bus, or they walked away to their homes. Most teachers left soon after the kids left, but some stayed to finished grading paperwork or go over lesson plans. But by the time the most meticulous teacher left, Era was still there in the parking lot. Staring forward in silence.

After Era realized the sun went down, she shook her head, took control of her thoughts, and made a decision.

"Goddamn. I need a fucking drink." She thought to

herself.

She drove to the Black Elysium, trying to stay calm and composed, processing her chaotic unspoken thoughts and emotions. A short drive later, she parked, grabbed something from the glove compartment to put into her pockets, got out of her car and entered.

She had hoped to see Arrow at the counter, but it looked like it was one of his days off. Instead, she ordered a drink from a different bartender. A slender woman in her mid-20s. She would often see her flirting with Arrow but scurried away whenever him and Era would start to talk. She slammed down a couple drinks back-to-back until she had enough courage to make an attempt at some social interaction.

20 minutes of arguing with herself on who to approach and Era saw more people coming in as the sun went down. Groups of friends that clearly were out for a good time, a couple loners, some couples having a date night, and some cretins just looking to get laid. The alcohol had slowly begun to make her feel a bit more adventurous, and less worried about Ranyo. She debated approaching a group of people that looked friendly.

Pepe had come in and replaced the woman at the bar.

"Oh hey, Era! Sorry fo Arrow not workin' today. He don said sum about a poem or sum shit. Watcha drinkin?"

Era asked for more screwdrivers to gain the courage to talk to the group. After spending too much, she finally approached one of the groups of friends. Walking quickly and stopping suddenly as soon as she got to their table.

"Umm… Hi. Do you think I could join you guys?" Era asked, one hand holding her arm while sustaining a light smirk.

Some of the group looked at Era with an amused shock, some with a look of reluctant surprise. But most of them had a look of welcoming sympathy.

"Sure, you can!" Stated one of the men in the group.

"Hi!" Welcomed one of the girls in the group. "Let me guess, you're a freshman at university and trying to get out?"

"Well, I'm actually a 3rd year." Era answered, "Ima... uhhh… I'm just trying to be a bit more social. My name is Era, it's short for Erebus."

One of the men raised his eyebrow. "Erebus? Like the Greak god of darkness?"

Era had no idea what he was talking about. "Ummm, I'm not sure to be honest. I never really met my real parents, and they're the ones that named me. Who knows why they named me that?"

One of the other girls gasped as she ogled Era arms and knuckles.  "Oh my god! You look so strong! Do you work out?!" She exclaimed as she reached out and started caressing Era's biceps. She was clearly intoxicated.

"Wellll… I do train at the boxing gym close to here. I used to compete." Era began sweating slightly at the current social banter being given. "I was in the lightweight class as a teenager." When Era said this, most of her awkwardness disappeared. Speaking of her abilities always seemed to give her confidence. After the girl ogled and complimented Era more, she began feeling confident enough to start flexing her biceps and showing off her aesthetic. And the girl began rubbing her hands all over Era's arms while the rest of the group laughed.

The rest of the night was spent in more screwdrivers and even some shots. Talking about a variety of subjects and life stories. The man that asked about her name was a theology major, the girl that complimented her was a physical therapy major. Some were engineers, others business majors. Era felt that she successfully broken out of her shell.

The night ended and they all decided to head out. Most took cabs, a couple has designated drivers. "Would you like a ride, Era?", one of them asked.

"I live closh… but shank you." Slurred Era. In an attempt to regain her composure, she pinched the skin above her nose and smiled. The alcohol was still affecting her. "I'll see you guys around. Maybe around school." Era told the others. They all smiled and went their ways.

Era turned around and started walking home, choosing not to drive. Feeling a small victory from successfully approaching strangers, she gave a slight grin and noticed she had a slight skip in her step. Every step was a step of conquest in her mind.

But. She noticed some small sounds coming from behind her. A light, but ugly consistent panting. She took a quick glance behind her and noticed someone behind her. Not thinking much of it, she continued, choosing to hold on to her recent victory. But as she kept walking, she noticed the sounds of the persons panting getting closer.

Paranoid, yet no longer the scared type, she turned around. "Can I fucking help you?" she aggressively asked the person. Her intoxication exacerbated her annoyance.

The person looked like someone from the bar. Either one of the loners she passively caught looking at her or someone from one of the groups who also seemed to give her some distant attention. As she stared him down, she reached both of her hands into her pockets and grabbed 2 rigid items.

The man moved forward and tried to grab her wrist. Bad move. Era quickly avoided his attempt at restraining her as she took her hands out of her pockets to expose the brass knuckles she had put on while reaching into her pockets.

She gave a quick 1,2 combo, punching him right on the bridge of the nose, breaking it. He let out a cry and from a distance some of what seemed to be his friends came running.

Two of them tried tackling Era. She was able to avoid the first man clumsily lunging at her in a pathetic attempt at a double leg, but she couldn't avoid the other. Era was skilled but being tacking by someone 100 pounds more than you takes a toll. After the impact, the man landed on top of her and pressed his larger hands against the side of her head to restrain her. The other man that missed his attempt at tackling her started ripping at her jeans while the man with the broken nose got up, walked towards her and cocked his fist back.

A flashback to Era's younger days. An older boy in primary school trying to kiss her as she continuously pushed him away. Era couldn't help but be distracted by this unwelcomed memory. But she quickly regained her composure and kicked the one tearing her jeans and punched the other in the crotch as she was on the ground. She then got up and gave the man that tacked her a 1-2-3 combo, breaking his nose and cheek bone, and a vicious right hook to the jaw of the one pawing at her jeans, quickly flattening him out. Each time she felt the brass knuckles connecting with one of her attackers body, she felt a slight crack in their bones. She calmy got up and looked at the 3 weak men with a piercing gaze that could stab body armor.

Era was too preoccupied with her attackers to realize that a girl holding a baseball bat came to the aid of the 3 men as the scuffle was taking place. Era caught her cocking the weapons back in her peripherals just in time to duck as she swung. After missing, the woman swung again; aiming for Era's head.

Being the elusive fighter that she was, Era once again ducked and avoided the swing. After the woman lost her footing in her unskilled attempt at hitting Era, she gave her a smooth right hook right to her lower jaw. Era felt another small crack during the connection right before the woman dropped to the floor. Her jaw was definitely broken, if not shattered. Putting the brass knuckles in her pockets before she went into the bar was a good idea.

The 3 men all watched as the woman that attacked got up. Her jaw seemed to be hanging from on side. One of them wiped the blood from his nose, while the other two looked in confusion as Era stared them down and put up her hands and took a stance, ready to attack and defend.

"STAY AWAY FROM ME!" Era yelled.

They couldn't even refuse while bleeding through their broken noses and all took a step back. Era took that as an 'ok.' Two of the men helped the woman that tried attacking Era with a bat and carried her away.

Era looked down and saw a lot of blood, mostly from her attackers covering the sidewalk. Plenty had made its way onto her brass knuckles as well. She made sure not to swing her fists with full force while wearing them, to avoid breaking her hand. She took them off, tore off a piece of her shirt and wiped herself of whatever blood was on her, and her weapons.

Now in a horrendous mood, Era continued walking home. But it wasn't the group that put her in a bad mood. It was the quick freezing up at the unwelcome memory from her younger days that upset her. One of the reasons she decided to take up boxing to begin with. She hated that she briefly let it stun her. But she brushed it off and attempted her usual routine as soon as she got home.

She tried eating but was unable to swallow her food. With every bite her immediate reaction was to vomit. After several attempts of consuming her food, she eventually gave up and chucked the food in the trash.

She marched towards her shower. Her dead eyes looking down as the shower head began `shooting down water and the mirror fogging up from the heat of Era's chosen temperature. She eventually gathered herself, undressed and got in.

As the water hit her skin, she let out slight gasps of pain. She sustained a few open wounds from the attacks and was unable to ignore the blood dripping down from the wounds as the water ran down her bare skin. Becoming even more irritated, she proceeded to quickly wash her body and exited the bathroom.

Era put on her sleeping attire and with a stern, blank look on her face. Several repressed memories kept forcing their way into her brain and she continuously tried blocking them out while she prepared to sleep. Another thought arose in her head; a hope of the Sage teaching her something again.

A quick fleeting plan to cease her existence crossed her mind as she slipped into her slumber. A plan that had been made multiple times before. A different form of an all-too-familiar feeling. Her head hit her pillow, and she drifted back into her dream-world.

# Part 2

# "The bullet in my head had writing on it"

Era found herself standing in front of a beat up, rundown house. A house similar to where she lived as a child. Broken windows, shattered bottles on the lawn, a car picked apart in the driveway and little dried-up pools of blood all over the cement.

She tried to turn away, but the house would move in front of her as she turned. She tried to take a step back, but the house would move closer to her, preventing any more distance between the two. She quickly turned her back and sprinted in the opposite direction, but the house lunged at her and swallowed her in through the front door.

Era looked at the back end of the front door and realized that she had been swallowed by the house. Realizing she was trapped, she turned and faced inside, looking into the hallways. Then she turned her head side to side looking into the living room, seeing blood spattered carpet and furniture. To her other side, a kitchen. She let out a slight gasp of reluctant recollection as she looked at a bloody knife and handprints on the floor and cupboards.

Little silhouettes the size of children laid on the floors and walls of the living room area. Some in the fetal position, some standing in the corner while facing inwards, and some laying lifeless with bloody mouths.

Era walked towards the hallways, reaching out for the

doorknobs on each door she could see. She called out for the Sage, frantically looking around in every room hoping he would save her from this nightmare. Her heart rate rose to a life-threatening speed, palms sweating, head throbbing. Clumsily slipping as she ran from door to door.

Era continued checking every room, but no matter how many rooms she checked, the Sage was nowhere to be found. And every time she opened a door, something seemed to change. As if the house was deliberately keeping her from finding what she wanted. A house with an infinite number of rooms, each with nothing in it, yet no two were similar.

Tears began to form in the corners of her eyes until she heard a door creak. She looked back and saw a brightly colored door amidst the constant unlit blackness of the house. She felt a small spark of hope and she slowly walked towards this beacon of happiness. She slowly turned the doorknob and poked her head into the room and looked inside. But what she saw caused her eyes to widen while her pupils shrank into the size of a pin.

A body, lifeless and beginning to rot. The body of a little girl named Erebus in the corner of the room. One arm hugging her knees and the other drooped on the floor, her palm facing up. Era walked towards the little girl and saw the cause of her death. A trail of blood leading up to her wrists. And as Era looked closer at her wrists, she saw that the little girl had carved words into her skin where the blood was coming out of. Carvings that read, *"Have faith"*. She remembered the reality that her younger self was currently in. That reality that she was so desperate to escape from. In whatever way possible.

Era slowly backed away and headed back towards the hallways of the hellish nightmare of a house. As she began to exit the room, she reached back to shut the door, but felt nothing. She turned around and saw that the room was gone. Vanished into thin air. Utterly terrified to look forward, she swallowed and turned around. And there was another door. Colored the same color as her door when she was a teenager. Reluctant to even move, let alone towards the door, the house hallways nudged her inside. And as she looked inside, she let out a light gasp as her now pale colored hands covered her mouth.

The overdosed body of a teenage girl named Erebus laying in the middle of the room. A bottle of prescription strength narcotics held tightly in her rigid hands that she had stolen from someone she knew. She walked towards her own teenage corpse and saw the labels of the bottle. But the labels didn't state the name of the drug that killed her. Instead, it read, *"Believe in yourself"*. Era remembered when she was planning this as well. A time where her foster parents would constantly belittle her vocation and Era had no one to rely on.

She paused for a second and turned around. Once again, slowly walking towards the hallway. She exited the room and saw another brightly colored room. Horrified, but knowing the house would force her in, she skittishly walked into the next room. And as she made her way inside, what she saw caused her to drop to her hands and knees and vomit uncontrollably.

Her own body. Hers. On the floor, with bits of her psyche splattered on the walls and floor. Blood amassed in a puddle right next to the exit wound on her temple. Her lifeless body still warm and limp from the freshness of the death, not yet overtaken by time and rigor mortis. After retching the last bit of water she had left in her pseudo stomach, she looked up. Wincing from the pain of excreting next to nothing, she saw the smoking pistol in her corpses hand. And next to the barrel was a hot shell that encased the projectile. She crawled forward and saw that the shell had writing on it that read, *"Never give up"*.

And Era realized that this was her plan not but a few hours ago.

# Chapter 8

## Part 1

Era woke up the next morning on the floor at the foot of her bed. All of her covers and blankets were on the floor as well, with the corner of one of them clenched up in her hands. The pillows were a near the opposite wall, about as far as she could throw from her bed. Her small twin mattress was still on the bedframe, but just barely. Era looked up at her alarm clock and saw that it was an hour passed her typical wake up time. The alarm didn't go off.

She got up and stumbled to her restroom and walked in front of the sink to look at her reflection. Her eyes were bloodshot with enormous bags underneath. She wasn't sure if it was from drinking the night prior, or from the god-awful nightmare she had. Her entire face looked exhausted; she still had those open wounds from her attackers. Era looked down at her forearms and saw some seemingly new scratch marks. But these seemed to be self-inflicted, probably from clawing at herself during her nightmare.

She looked back up to the mirror to take another look at herself. Her hair a mess, her loose-fitting pajama shirt almost torn in half, bloody, and all around defeated and miserable looking. She almost let a small tear get away before she took in a deep breath and dried her eyes.

Today was a fully loaded day, so Era couldn't let anything get in the way of working and needed to hurry to make class. She quickly put on her usual clothes, black t-shirt, jeans, and her black combat boots, quickly brushed her hair and got her school things ready. But there was one thing she needed to do that she doesn't typically work on. Some makeup specifically to cover up her facial bruising. It took a little longer than when she used to when she was a kid, seeing it has been years since she had to. But it was good enough. Although nothing could be done about the wounds on her arm.

She eventually finished up, got her things, headed out the door, got in her car and started driving to campus. Traffic was worse than when Era typically drives. It seems she just hit the early morning rush hour. She drove calmly but was gripping the wheel tight enough to make the veins on her hand pop out.

After a longer drive than she was used to, she eventually arrived at her typical parking spot. But it was taken, so she had to drive a bit further back to find another one. A 2-minute drive later, she found one. She parked, and stiffly got out of her car to head to class. She glanced down at her watch and saw that she was going to end up being 10 minutes late. But that fact didn't cause her to walk faster. She kept her breathing calm and began a slow-paced walk.

20 minutes later, she walked into the class as it was being held. Professor Sigmund was in the middle of speaking as Era opened the door. Normally she would hide her face and skittishly walk to an open seat if she was late, but her level of fucks given was next to 0 and she remained stern faced as she took a seat and took out her note taking

equipment.

The class was indifferent to Era being late. Which was good, considering Era would more than likely lose her temper if anyone said anything about it during her current state. Her mind was blank. A fiery anger that burned away frivolous thoughts gave her focus. And that focus helped her soak in every single word that Professor Sigmund spoke.

Her pencil as fast as your average programmer could type, Era jotted down everything that the professor was saying. The main topic of the class was about the psychoanalytic concept of repression. As Era understood it, it is a person going through something so traumatic and painful, that a person blocks it out by shoving it deep into their unconscious and typically become unaware of whatever took place. Unfortunately, that repressed memory or emotions can still manifest itself through actions without the person realizing it.

As Era kept taking notes, the Professor briefly stopped talking and writing on the chalkboard, then turned to face the class.

"What do you think is the best way to help someone that has repressed memories or emotions? Uhhhh… you. What do you think?" The Professor said as he pointed at one of the students raising her hand.

Era turned to look at the person the Professor had chosen to answer and saw that it was Anabel. The big haired girl with glasses that asked her for some advice years ago.

"The best thing to do with someone dealing with any type of repression is probably to slowly face their repression until they can overcome what happened. That's what I think, professor." Said the girl with glasses, now speaking with a professional powerful energy rather than being timid. She seemed to be handling things much better now. She didn't look exhausted, nor on the verge of tears.

"Very good." Said the Professor before calling on another student. "What about you?"

Several other students gave their answers. Some suggested medication, some suggested a passive approach, and some suggested cognitive therapy. But the girl with glasses' answer stuck with Era in particular.

One raised his hand to ask a question. "Professor, if someone doesn't realize that they even have repressed memories or emotions because they are too painful to deal with, what's the problem with letting them keep it repressed?"

The professor stopped his pacing of the classroom, faced the students and sternly responded, "I want you all to keep in mind, that the failure to deal with repression can sometimes cause people to act out and become mentally ill, sometimes becoming something they themselves hate. The psyche will deal with it whether directly, or indirectly. Sometimes, you can tell a person has repressed rage because they get angry at little, meaningless things, or repressed sadness because they cry over seemingly trivial things. Repressed memories of abuse can sometimes cause someone to become their abuser, as an outlet.”

Era jotted down every word he said.

After a few more answers from students regarding what to do when dealing with repression, the professor decided to end the class.

Era quickly gathered her things and headed out of the class to her next one. She maintained her focus and calm demeanor as she took a casually paced walk to her next class.

About halfway down the hallway, she heard some quick footsteps coming up from behind her.

“BOO!!!” She heard as she felt a hand on her shoulder. But rather than the usual jumpy reaction Era would give Arrow for his silly pranks, she simply stared at him. Clearly unamused.

If Era hadn’t recognized the footsteps, she would have immediately turned around and broke the nose of whoever it was that attempted to scare her.

Arrow’s usual happy grin turned into a deep look of concern as he saw Era’s face.

“Dude, what’s wrong?” He asked.

“Nothing, I just am really not in the mood.” A few years ago, she would have told Arrow to fuck off, but she was trying to control the Hellstorm. They both continued walking, although it was only Arrow trying at any conversation.

Arrow looked at Era's arms and noticed the red marks and scrape wounds on her shoulders before looking at her face.

"Era, you're wearing a lot more makeup than usual, are you ok?" Era heard that Arrow's tone of voice was genuinely concerned and didn't want to take any of her frustration out on him. She walked off to a bit of an excluded area on the walkway to the next class and waved Arrow over.

"Look…" Era started. "I had a really bad night last night. I don't want to take it out on anyone, but I really need to be alone right now. Ok?"

Arrow looked slightly hurt by Era's words but accepted them.

"Ok, Era…" He said. "Hit me up when you're ok to talk again. Be safe."

Arrow turned and walked away and went into the stream of students walking from building to building. Era took a deep breath, waited for Arrow to walk out of sight and eventually continued her way onto her next class.

Era's mood had slightly improved since hearing Arrows concerned voice, but it wasn't nearly enough to quell her anger. Her anger continued giving her focus as she continued her slow-paced walk to the next class.

A short while later, she arrived. She was 15 minutes

early, so she decided to go over the notes before the class would start. After organizing her things in front of her, she grazed over them and watched as the students started walking in one by one. Professor Fredrich taught this class as well and would be going over abstract philosophical concepts today.

During the class, the professor went over things regarding unpleasant truths that some people may reject. The concepts were oddly similar to the concepts in Professor Sigmund class on repression. Some of the concepts were about the value of being hurt, and that suffering can help people ascertain virtue. And that living meant you would inevitably suffer and overcoming the suffering can help one find themself.

"Keep in mind, class. That whoever fights monsters, should be careful not to become one themselves. And if you gaze long enough into the abyss, the abyss will gaze into you as well." Professor Fredrich explained.

As Era wrote this down on her notepad, a student raised his hand to ask a question.

"Professor, what exactly does that mean?" He asked.

After hearing the question, Professor Fredrich smiled, moved to the front of his desk, leaned back against it and began stroking his absurdly long mustache. "Let's let someone else answer that. This is a philosophy class, after all. Would anyone like to volunteer?"

One student raised his hand and answered. "I think it means that you can become what you hate if you're not careful."

Another student raised her hand and answered, "I think it means that an unpleasant truth can hurt you if you're not ready for it."

A vet turned student gave another answer. "It could be a soldier reference. Fighting in wars can make you become something horrible".

Several students gave their different answers, and Era wrote down all of them, taking all of their perspectives into consideration. They answered continuously until the designated class time was over, and Professor Fredrich dismissed the class.

Era had the day off from work, since the primary school gave the kids a half day. Whenever she had extra time to herself due to no work, she would take the time to either study or train. Considering she didn't want to be around people, she chose the latter.

Era made her way from the campus, weaving her way through the streams of students and eventually making her way to her car, parked further than she was used to. She got in and drove to the training center. Still focused.

After a short time driving, Era arrived and quickly made her way in. In less than 5 minutes, she walked in, changed, wrapped up her hands, and was in the punching bag area. Not even bothering to warm up, she started hammering the first bag she came across with a flurry of power hooks and crosses.

Everyone in the bag area looked to Era, hearing the audible SMACKS with every strike. Jab, cross, hook. SMACK, SMACK, SMACK. Triple right side hooks. SMACK, SMACK, SMACK. Cross, hook, cross. SMACK, SMACK, SMACK. The other members looked in pity to the poor bags Era was punishing, hoping they would last the next few minutes.

Era continued wailing on the bag, until she heard some familiar heavy steps coming up behind her. She stopped and turned to face him.

"Ey girly, take it easy on tha bag work!" Cassius said. "Yo gon end up hurtin' yoself. Didya even bother warmin up?"

"Noooo…" Era sighed.

As she said no, she noticed a slight ache in her shoulder and elbow tendons and gripped her right shoulder with her left hand as she moved her arm in a circular motion to get some blood flowing.

"Ya see? I done told ya to warm up before ya start beatin the shit out of these here bags." Cassius said.

Era took a step back, took off her gloves and started doing her proper warmups before she would continue her bag work.

"If ya wanna do summin, do it right." Cassius said as he walked away, leaving Era to her previous activities.

Era continued warming up, doing some low rep

pushups, arm circles and various other dynamic stretches until her irritating pain was gone, then she continued wailing on the bags as she was before.

Jab, cross, hook, uppercut. SMACK, SMACK, SMACK, SMACK. Triple hook, jab, cross. SMACK, SMACK, SMACK, SMACK, SMACK. Cross, hook, hook. SMACK, SMACK, SMACK. Era's therapy went on for an hour, until Cassius invited Era over for some sparring. He paired her with the same rookie as last time. But Era held her anger back enough to give the rookie only a mild beating.  Plenty of parries, ducks, bruising, and loud smacks later, Cassius told Era that they were done for the day, and she went to shower and change over. Ready to go home. She began walking towards the exit until she heard Cassius call her name.

"ERA!" He yelled.

Era stopped and turned to face him as he walked up to her. "Ey, girly. I didn' wanna say anythin earlier in front of tha kids, but I recognize a jumpin when I see one. What happened?"

Era just looked down in shame, unwilling to speak about it.

"Girly, I remembr' how ya use to come to this gym after school. Ya wouldn' wanna leave. And I recognize those ole bruises and cuts, just like I recognize you hidin bruises neath' that makeup now. Ya can't keep runnin from what happend', girly. "An remember, whoever isn willin ta take risks will nevr' accomplish anythin' in life."

Era stood there, silent but listening. "I know ya can take care a yurself, but just be careful. Am always aroun' if you need summin. G' night." Cassius patted Era on the head as he headed out.

Era stood in that same spot for a couple minutes. Lost in a sea of thoughts about nothing. Until she finally took a deep breath, headed out the door, got in her car, and drove home.

When Era got to her little studio, she totally ignored her routine. She walked through her front door, firmly shut it behind her, threw all her things on the floor, quickly undressed, took some sleeping medicine and threw herself on top of her sheetless mattress and knocked out hard.

## Part 2

### "The difference between pessimism and optimism"

Era opened her eyes, and as her vision came into focus, a blurred vision of a masked man wearing a hoodie standing 10 feet in front of her became clear.

Era clenched her fists and gritted her teeth as she took aggressive steps towards the Sage. With every step closer, her fists clenched harder. After she was an arm's length away, she hit him on his mask-covered face with a right cross. She hated that he wasn't there when she needed him.

The Sage rolled with the punch. She took a step back,

got in her fighting stance and lunged at the Sage to attack again. Era hit the Sage in the ribs with some body hooks. The Sage stood there motionless, taking every strike in silence, making Era even more angry.

Era continued to throw punches at the Sage. Her hair swaying with every swing, nostrils flaring, gritted teeth, and eyes on the verge of tears. She switched from body shots to uppercuts to his chin, and power hooks to strike him across the mask. After punching for just under a minute, Era started to run out of breath and took a step back.

Era stood there with her fists still clenched, now dripping with blood. Her breathing erratic and face flushed red with anger. The Mask was harder than she thought it would be, and her knuckles were paying the price for those punches. The Sage continued to stand there in silence, unfazed.

After calming herself down, Era's eyes slowly became blurry again from tears and she rushed to hug the Sage. She left a small trail of blood that was dripping from her knuckles.

"WHERE- WHERE- WHERE-"

Era couldn't control her speech beneath her crying and gasping as tears ran down her face.

"WHERE..."

With each stuttered word spoken, Era's arms gripped the Sage tighter. And as he wrapped his arms around her back, she buried her face into his chest and finally was able to articulate some words.

"WHERE WERE YOU LAST NIGHT!?!" Era screamed. "I WAS SO SCARED AND I NEEDED YOU THERE WITH ME IN THAT FUCKING HOUSE!!"

The Sage placed his hands on Era's cheeks and lifted her face up to look directly into his angry and smiling mask. He wiped her tears with his thumbs and took a deep breath.

"I'm sorry, Era. I'm not allowed in that house. As soon as it swallowed you, we were separated indefinitely. I wanted to help you so bad, but I wasn't able to."

Era's tears kept running down her cheeks, but the deep and calm soothing voice of the Sage calmed her down, but she still gave an occasional stutter in her sentences.

"I guess- I guess- this is another thing- thing- that I won't really under- understand for now, huh? Era asked.

The Sage placed both of his hands on Era's shoulders.

"Don't worry about that for now." Said the Sage. "Now dry your tears and take a deep breath."

Era did as instructed, and wiped the tears and snot from her face, closed her eyes and inhaled deeply. She was still in crying mode, so had to take several deep breaths until she was able to fully stop. Once she did, she wiped her face with her hands one last time and looked at the Sage.

"Are you ready, Era?" Asked the Sage.

Era gave an unsure grin and answered. "Yes."

The Sage turned around and waved his hand to signal Era to follow him. As the Sage walked forward a few meters ahead of her, Era composed herself and hurriedly walked towards him to catch up. The two walked on in silence for a few minutes until the Sage began to speak.

"That was horrible what happened, Era. It's bad enough that Ranyo got taken away by those agents, but then you got jumped by random people just looking to cause trouble,"

Era looked down and grabbed her arm.

"It's ok, Era. I know exactly how you feel." Said the Sage as he put his hand on her shoulder while walking. "And I especially know why it bugged you so much. It reminded you of what you went through." Era felt her eyes begin to lightly water again as she gripped her arm even tighter.

The two walked on for a bit longer until they finally reached yet another cliff. Era saw two beings wearing cloaks that covered their entire body and hid their faces. Both were looking down into whatever was at the bottom of the cliff.

A sudden wave of thunderclouds filled the skies, and a heavy rain started while a steady stream of wind began throwing Eras hair up. The wind was strong enough to blow the bottom of the two beings' cloaks to their sides, but they remained totally covered.

As Era and the Sage walked closer and closer, Era began to see the edge of the thing that was at the bottom of the cliff. And as they got closer still, it became abundantly clear.

The abyss.

Era didn't want to look into it. But she could see the two beings looking directly into the abyss with the utmost focus. Staring directly into it, as if they were challenging it.

Era turned her head to look at the Sage and asked. "Who are they?"

The Sage tilted his head to look down to Era.

"This…" The Sage started. "Is pessimism and optimism."

And as the Sage said this and pointed at the two, both beings looked at Era. And a quick flash of lightning followed by a roar of thunder exposed the faces hidden under their hoods. They each wore one of the Thalia and Melpomene masks. Pessimism wore the mask of tragedy, and optimism wore the mask of comedy.

After Era looked at them both long enough to get a good look at each mask, the two looked back down into the abyss, refocusing their attention on it.

"Do you know what's down there, Era?" Asked the Sage.

Era glanced back down and gave it a little bit of thought.

"It's an abyss." Answered Era.

"This is the abyss that most people throw their forsaken truths and past into, Era." Explained the Sage. "It has all of it in there. Pain, trauma, and a lack of purpose, lies."

Era glanced down and noticed the abyss move.

"But look at how each of these two reacts to the abyss, Era." Said the Sage as he pointed Era at the two as an instruction to look.

Era looked at the two, both still staring downward into the abyss. Both seemed to accept it, know it, and believe in it.

Era heard a small rumbling at the bottom of the cliff, and in the corner of her eyes, she saw that the abyss started moving and shifting around and formed what seemed to be the shape of a giant eye. And suddenly, she felt the abyss give a piercing and powerful look at the two beings. Suddenly the being called pessimism looked away and fell to its knees, unable to stand. But optimism did not flinch and remained standing, returning the abyss the same stare it had been giving this entire time.

"Do you see the difference between the two, Era?" Asked the Sage. "They both look at the same thing and have the same beliefs. They both accept and know the abyss. But the difference between pessimism and optimism is, one remains strong in the face of that very abyss. The other crumbles."

And as Era heard the Sage speak, the clouds overhead

went away, and the rain stopped. Optimism helped Pessimism back up to its feet and the two walked away as the abyss disappeared into itself.

Then the Sage placed his hand on Era's shoulder.

"Era." He started. "We need to go back to that Hellhouse."

Era's eyes widened and her jaw slightly dropped as she began hyperventilating. She hugged her arms and started recoiling into a fetal position.

But the Sage stood in front of her and once again placed his hands on her shoulders, picking her up to stand up straight.

"Take a deep breath, Era." He said. "You can face it."

The two began walking away from the cliff towards their intended destination. After a short while of a slow-paced walk coupled with silence, Era saw the same black house with an evil spirit from her nightmare the night before. As Era walked closer, she felt another urge to drop to her knees and vomit, but the Sage kept her from collapsing.

They continued closer and closer until they were in front of it. The Sage placed his hand on Era's back and gently pushed her forward so she could face it close up.

"Remember the difference between the two Era." Said the Sage.

As Era stood in front of the hell house, it opened its door

to reveal what was inside. An abyss full of blood-stained walls, Era's corpses, overdosed, hanging from a ceiling, slit wrists, shattered bottles, and torn pieces of clothing on the floor. The house lunged forward as if to devour Era as it did before.

But rather than run away as Era did before, she stood still. Her pulse racing, her eyes forward and focused, and standing firm.

The house stopped right in front of Era, Realizing Era was not flinching, it backed up and lunged forward again, opening its door for a second time to reveal the atrocities inside. But Era once again, did not flinch.

The hell house receded once more and began to change. The front door and windows remained open. The blood on the walls began to disappear, Era's corpses turned into plushies that placed themselves in the corner. The shattered glasses put themselves in the trash, and the hellish aura and demonic presence so abundant in this place suddenly became a distant and accepted memory.

# Chapter 9


## "Fake Tattoos and a shotgun you can't hold right"


Another semester had passed, and Era was continuously progressing in her classes as she had been these last couple years. Today was the first day of another summer, but Era had a couple weeks' worth of free time before she took her university summer classes and helped Miss Magist with the primary school summer lessons.

Her usual strict routine of getting her blood flowing, stretching, and eating her health-oriented breakfast in a timely manner was nonexistent for this couple of weeks. Rather, she would turn off her alarm and sleep in until the late morning and indulge in pancakes or waffles for her first meal. This period of rest was sure to do her well.

After waking up, wiping the drool off her face, and stumbling to her mirror, she'd straighten out her hair and figure out what she would do for the day, besides train in the evening.

The previous years, her free time were spent doing preemptive studying for the classes she knew she would be taking, extra training, going to spoken words with Arrow, spending time at Elysium, or sometimes a day of sleeping in and doing nothing.

Era decided to change it up and take a stroll at the mall. Maybe do some people watching and do a bit of shopping for new clothes. After fully waking up and eating, she got her things, headed out, got in her car, and drove off.

Waking up a little later than usual allowed her to avoid the usual morning rush, so she was able to drive at a leisurely pace. After arriving, she parked her car and headed inside.

The Mall didn't have a lot of vehicles in the parking lot, so she was able to park close. The first store she saw was a bookstore, so that's the first place she would go inside of. Books weren't typically her vocation unless they were college assignments, like the ones that Professor Fredrich would assign the class. But she went inside anyways.

The shopkeeper was a tall pale man, with a thick mustache and parted black hair. He wore a defeated look on his face. His nametag read 'Edward Poe'.

"Hello, ma'am." He greeted. "Is there any genre I can interest you in today?"

"I'm not sure." Era answered.

The shopkeeper stood there and looked back into the different sections of books and pointed to the 3rd aisle.

"If you're new to literature and just want something easy to read, you could try out the poetry section." Mr. Poe said.

And suddenly Era thought of getting Arrow a small

present that she thought may help him with his spoken word events.

"Thank you!" Era said as she walked towards the aisle. She grazed a few different books that had an amalgam of short stories and poems. Ranging from poems about a woman named Lee and Ravens of grief. Era eventually picked a couple, bought them, and headed out. She was looking forward to gift them to Arrow as soon as she could.

Era strolled down the mall passing several stores, and occasionally went into one to check out what was inside. A sports store where she would check if they had any boxing equipment or dumbbells, a clothing store for more baggy shirts to wear to sleep, and jeans to replace the ones that were wore out.  During her grazing in a dress store, Era noticed a cocktail dress with an 'on sale' sign. She waved down one of the store representatives to ask about the dress.

"Oh, that dress is on sale because no one wants to buy it, ma'am."

"Why not?" Era asked

"Well ma'am, mostly because people don't enjoy wearing something all black during the summer. And on top of that, it's very revealing. It shows the midriff, barely covers the legs, and has a small section that exposes the middle of the chest. But I'll tell you what, ma'am. If you buy it, I'll throw in a pair of high heels along with it. I really need this space for new items."

Era took the rep up on his offer.

She continued strolling and shopping, but a small commotion in her path at one of the stores caught her attention. The sign above the entrance read 'Tajimamori Candy Shop'. She kept walking and feeling nosey, she decided to check out was going on.

After looking inside, she saw that it was Rusty and Miss Magist talking to a security guard in front of the cashier. Rusty had a sour look on his face and Miss Magist seemed worried. The cashier and security guard had a frustrated look on their face.

Era walked up to them in an attempt to interact with the group, but the security guard quickly moved in front of her path to stop her. He was balding, fat, and had a high-pitched voice.

"Excuse me, ma'am. Please be on your way."

Era ignored him and called out to Miss Magist

"What's going on?" Era asked.

Miss Magist took a deep sigh while looking Era in the eye.

"Rusty got caught trying to shoplift some candy. ISN'T THAT RIGHT?" She sternly asked Rusty while giving him an intense, piercing look.

Rusty crossed his arms, looked away, and gave a childish, "Yes."

The cashier chipped in. "I'm sorry, ma'am, but store policy is not to tolerate shoplifting. Either the security guard takes him to the security office, or someone pays for the product, and he be banned from this store.”

“Is that it?” Era asked. “I’ll pay for it, and we can just get out of here.”

Miss Magist walked towards Era and moved in close to her ears so that the cashier and security guard couldn’t hear her. “Rusty has a pistol in his pocket. I stopped him from pulling it out as the cashier caught him lifting the candy, so keep an eye on him.”

Era pulled her head back in shock but managed to keep her composure to prevent any suspicion from the security guard and cashier.

“So how much was it?” Era asked. “We’ll just pay for it and be on our way.”

Rusty kept silent the entire time. Era glanced at his arms and noticed he had a bunch of drawings on his arms from a pen that was clearly running out of ink. An obvious attempt at giving himself something that resembled tattoos.

After a bit of back and forth, Era paid the fee. The cashier took a picture of Rusty to put on the ‘never allowed in’ wall and the three went on their way.

“Let’s go outside.” Said Miss Magist. “I don’t want anyone to hear what I’m going to say.”

The three walked towards the exit where Era had entered from. After stepping outside, Miss Magist pulled Rusty to one of the walls of the main building where no one was at.

"Rusty, give me the gun." Instructed Miss Magist.

Rusty gave a dumb founded look to pretend he wasn't aware of what Miss Magist was talking about.

Miss Magist gave Rusty a harsh look and crossed her arms.

"Rusty. I'm not stupid. I saw you reach into the back of your pants to try and pull it out as that security guard came up to you. Now. GIVE. IT. TO. ME."

Rusty looked down and reached into the back of his pants and pulled out a rusted over revolver with loose fitting rounds nestled in the chamber. The handle was too big for his hands, so he couldn't wrap his fingers around it, and he clearly didn't know where the trigger or hammer was located by the way he handled it. He held it out and as Miss Magist took hold of it, she burst into tears.

Era stepped forward to console her, but after a few seconds of hearing Miss Magist, she realized they were tears of laughter. She was laughing so hard that she was wheezing and crying.

After 30, stomach-aching seconds of laughter and Rusty looking embarrassed and red cheeked, Miss Magist composed herself and finally spoke.

"Rusty!" She gave little bits of laughter in between her words.

"Where did you even get this? These things probably

haven't been used since the dark ages! And the bullets you have inside don't even fit!" Miss Magist laughed hysterically.

"I dunno." Said Rusty. "I found it."

As Era wondered how Miss Magist knew all this, she suddenly had a flashback to a lunch where Era and Miss Magist shared stories about themselves. Era went on about her usual fighting days and how college classes were going. Miss Magist had told her that before she became a teacher, she had taught pistol shooting to the military before they deployed and was a regular part of shooting competitions as a young adult and had a plethora of firearms in her house. Her father was a captain in the Army and taught her everything she knew about guns.

Miss Magist continued her chuckles as light as possible as she lectured him. As Era looked at them both, she noticed a small welt sticking out from Rusty's t shirt. It looked like there was dried blood below it.

"Hold on, Miss Magist." Era interrupted. "Rusty, what is that under your shirt sleeve?"

Rusty held on to his shirt as he turned away.

"It's none of your fucking business!" Yelled Rusty.

Era looked at Rusty directly in the eyes but didn't lose her temper. Instead, she walked towards him and held him by his shoulders and gently said. "Let me see."

Rusty struggled slightly as Era held him still to look at

what was under his sleeve. It was a poorly done attempt at branding. In the shape of an R. Era assume it was for his name.

They seemed to be almost healed and not infected, save for some light bruising and scabbed over blood around it.

"Rusty, what have you been doing these past couple of weeks?"

"My parents let me do whatever I fucking want, so I go where I want and do whatever I want. They said they just want me out of the house."

As Rusty spoke, Era noticed his voice was starting to change. A few years after primary school and he was now in secondary school. Puberty was starting to hit him.

"And my dad said, if I want to be a man, I need to figure it out by myself. So, he told me to get out and get my own food."

Miss Magist and Era looked at each other.

"Rusty." Miss Magist started.

"Hold on." Interrupted Era. "I think I know where to take him." Era looked down to ask him a question. "Want to go somewhere pretty fun, Rusty?"

Rusty shrugged to signal 'I guess'.

Miss Magist agreed to whatever Era's plans were and left it at that.

"Ok, Era. Just keep him safe."

Miss Magist went on her own way as Era and Rusty headed to her car. Both of them remained silent during the walk. They remained silent during the ride as well. After a 20-minute drive, they arrived at their destination. HallaVal martial arts.

Era told Rusty to get out. Rusty was giving Era attitude with every order she gave him. Either looking away, rolling his eyes, or putting his hands to his ears to block out her words. Era refused to lose her temper and remained calm and collected.

She guided him to the front desk. She explained the situation to the staff, and they let Rusty come in without a legal guardian.

The two made their way into the bag room and as Era saw coach Cassius instructing some other kids, she waved him down. After coming face to face, Era explained the entire situation, hoping Cassius could provide Rusty with some wisdom.

After hearing everything Era had to say about the situation, Cassius turned to Rusty, crossed his arms and sternly spoke.

"Oh, So ya think ya fuckin hard huh, ya lil punk?" Cassius said.

Rusty just looked up at him with a haughty look of defiance.

"Well if ya think ya so hard, why don't ya put on sum gloves and knuckle up with dis lil girl?" Cassius said as he pointed towards one of the boxing students. It was the rookie.

"If ya so tough, ya can handle it, huh?"

Rusty suddenly gave an arrogant look on his young puberty-stricken face as he nodded and agreed to try.

"I can easily take on a girl." He said with a cocky grin.

Cassius ordered Era to wrap up and equip young Rusty for a proper round, and Cassius instructed the young Rookie to show her opponent no mercy.

Era kept silent as she laced up Rusty. All the while, Rusty maintained this cocky I'll-show-you attitude as this all took place.

"I'm gonna put that little girl in her place!" Rusty yelled out before Era put in his mouthpiece.

Cassius gave a light chuckle.

Era shooed Rusty to enter the Ring, and coach Cassius told the young Rookie to enter as well. The two got in and the sparring bell rang loudly, echoing throughout the room.

The young protégé came in with several jabs, and Rusty; not knowing how to defend ate each strike. Rusty swung wildly in anger, to which the young boxer easily evaded with a weave and came up with a clean uppercut straight to Rusty's lip, cutting it open.

After getting his lip cut, Rusty covered himself to prevent any more shots from coming to contact with his face. But the young protégé effortlessly switched to body shots as Rusty stood there, acting as a punching bag.

The first bell rang, giving Rusty a chance to rest and think. Utterly confused as to what to do, all he could do was breathe hard and wait for the next round to come.

A minute later, they started again. Rusty's arrogant smirk now gone, he tried swinging wide again, to which his opponent easily evaded and gave him another uppercut as punishment for his ignorant swings. Another jab, jab, hook right to Rusty's head, causing him to become discombobulated and cover up in fear again. After another couple of flurries later, Rusty took one power hook to his head that caused him to crumble.

As he fell to the floor, he started getting teary eyed and let out little whines. Era went in between the ropes and entered the ring to help him. She picked him up by his shoulders and led him out of the ring. His opponent smiled from the other side of the ring, content that she put an arrogant talker in his place.

"By the way…" The rookie began. "My name isn't 'that little girl'. My name is Chikara! And I just whooped your ass!" Her taunting hurt Rusty almost as bad as the cuts he had on his face.

Era sat Rusty down on a stool and helped him take off his headgear and gloves. Then Era called for a first aid kit from one of the staff members, and after a few minutes it came. She worked to clean the blood from Rusty's nose and cuts on his mouth. Rusty winced at every touch near his cuts, causing his steady stream of tears to increase. Era heard some heavy footsteps from behind her. Recognizing it, she stood up and turned around.

"Ya almost done cleanin him up, girly?" Asked Cassius.

"Not yet, coach. I'm almost done." Answered Era.

"Aight, take ya time."

After applying some cleaning ointment and wiping any remaining blood from his face and covering his cuts with some skin adhesives, Era was done. She stood up and stepped to the side to let Coach Cassius talk to Rusty.

"Stand up, kiddo." Said Cassius.

Rusty reluctantly did as he was instructed to do. His entire stance screamed defeat and shame. He was looking down, slouched shoulders, and his eyes were on the verge of releasing tears again.

Cassius took on somewhat of a serious and less chilled out tone that usual. The same tone that he would give Era when she was a kid. Not using as much slang and speaking with a powerful voice that demanded you listen.

"You see, kiddo. You think you're being tough and fighting back against the world by acting like this, but all you're doing is hurting yourself even worse than the people that hurt you did. You think you're crazy, and you do things that you think makes you tough. But in reality, you're just scared to work hard and care about something. Because you're scared to get hurt."

Cassius continued talking to Rusty as Era walked away, letting them talk in private. She decided to get in some bag work herself, until Coach Cassius was done speaking to Rusty.

30 minutes, and a good sweat later, Era saw that Rusty and Cassius were done talking. They both walked up to Era, and she stopped punishing the bag to hear what they had to say.

Rusty no longer had a defeated look on his face, and Cassius was smiling.

"Welcome a new member to our team, Girly!"

# Chapter 10

## Part 1

The alarm went off, waking a sleepy and groggy Era up. After shutting off the alarm and sitting up, she wiped the slobber from the corners of her mouth and stretched. A semester had come and gone since Rusty joined the boxing team, and he was doing well, and she was seeing an improved attitude in him. All of her classes were essentially done, and she was acing every single course.

It was nearing towards the end of the semester. Finals were over, so most of the classes were extremely lackadaisical if not finished. Little to no homework in her classes and Miss Magist was planning an end of semester party for the younglings.

Today was a weekend day, and there was a rising senior's ceremony being held on campus for the college students that were entering their final year. Era had been debating for weeks what to wear to the ceremony, but the night prior decided to finally wear the on-sale cocktail dress she had bought the previous summer. This was definitely an occasion to wear it.

After pulling the sheets off her toned, smooth body she got out of bed and did her usual stretching and light blood flow for the mornings. She still had on her sleeping attire that consisted of nothing more than an oversized, loose-fitting shirt and a pair of cotton panties. She went with the typical pushups, pullups, squats, and curls. Just enough to incite a slight burn and a light sweat.

With every squat, her rock hard, thick thighs burned and let out little drops of sweat. With every push up her triceps flared out, showing a defined cut in each of her arms. With every pull up, her loose shirt would hike up as she came down, exposing her lightly defined abs. With every curl, a small vein would pop out of her chiseled bicep. After a few rounds, a pool of sweat had built on the tiled floors. A few veins in her arms were throbbing and her chest was feeling contracted from the pushups, causing her boobs to perk up a little more than usual.

Being content with her blood flow, Era walked towards the bathroom to wash her face and brush her teeth. She had a slight bit of leftover lip gloss from the previous day that made her lips glisten. Her skin was looking particularly impeccable, and despite having bed head, her hair was smooth and free a split-ends.

The rising senior's ceremony wouldn't start until midday, so Era took her time getting ready. After a long steaming hot shower that would burn Satan himself, she dried off and walked to her closet. The cocktail dress fit her perfectly and hugged her in all the right areas. After glancing in the mirror, Era realized why the store had trouble selling it. The tight fit was not suitable for everyone, but it went with Era's toned body very well. The jet-black color perfectly complimented her sun kissed skin and black hair. It also brought out the dark green color in her eyes in the most beautiful way.

After admiring how the dress showed off her tight legs

and how the midriff opening showed off her abs, she began putting on her makeup. Not in any type of rush, she perfectly applied the rose-colored lipstick and blush. Her impudent mother taught her something useful in a sea of mistakes and debauchery.

After a couple hours' worth of getting ready, Era put on the high heels she had got along with the dress and headed to the ceremony.

The event was being held outside in a large grassy area in the middle of the campus. The area was large enough for a couple hundred men and women to comfortably be in. The event was formal, so students and guests were encouraged to dress up and be respectful during the speeches. Round tables with white cloths were scattered all around the event area. Era's assigned seat was given to her alone with her invitation. Her seat number was 96. Era saw that most of the seats were empty. Probably from her being early.

After searching for and finding the table she was assigned to, a familiar face caught her eye.

"Hey dude!" Arrow yelled.

Era saw him sitting at seat 97 and gave a huge grin. "HHHIIIIIIIIII! Fancy meeting you here!"

Era sat down and the two began chatting away as more and more students came in. Arrow came dressed in the most formal attire she had ever seen him in. Rather than the usual t shirt and shorts, he was wearing a slick, fitted white dress shirt with a black sleeveless vest and black dress pants. His clothes perfectly brought out his bright sideways smile. He rolled his shirt sleeves up to his forearms, exposing his vascular arms and hands.

"So did you bring anyone for your plus one?" Arrow asked during the constant chattering.

"Pffft, no." Era replied. "I specifically told the staff I would be coming alone. What about you?"

Before Arrow got the chance to answer, a tall slender woman with long brown hair in a slick satin gown sat down at the table right next to Arrow.

"Yeah, actually." Said Arrow.

The woman stared intently at Arrow, waiting for him to finish his sentence.

"Oh." Era said while swallowing a bit of air. "So, you brought your girlfriend?"

Arrow let out a big sigh. "No. My older sister insisted she come to the party so she could meet some younger college guys."

The woman laughed and reached her hand out to Era. "Well can you blame me? Hi, my name is Hedone. Little Air has actually mentioned you a couple of times whenever he talks about school. Nice to meet you!"

Era reached out to shake her hand while internally letting out an enormous sigh of relief. Right after she and Hedone finished shaking hands, Era caught a glimpse of Arrow staring at her lower body right before glancing back up to look at her eyes. Era returned the favor.

The 3 conversed until the ceremony speeches commenced. A typical speech about the future success of students and some cliché statements about how much the students have sacrificed and worked to make it to the rising seniors ceremony. After the speeches and ceremonies were done, lines formed for food and music began for students to let loose and dance to. Many of the students were couples and took full advantage of the blaring music. Some students had significant others as their plus one, and others were simply going to classes together.

Era and Arrow joined in the festivities, eating, dancing, and indulging in some liquid courage at the open bar. Arrow had occasionally let his hand wander to the small of Era's back while they danced and the cologne he was wearing made her knees wobble every so often. Hedone danced with Era as well but went off to find other single college boys to dance with.

After a few hours, the festivities dwindled and most of the students had left and the sun started to go down, Hedone had picked her plaything for the next few weeks and pestered Arrow to leave.

They parted ways, and Era decided to go back to her studio to change and head to HallaVal for some light training.

Coach Cassius had told Era he wouldn't be at the gym during the weekend, but Era still decided to go. Just to get in a light workout and work on some form and mitting in preparation for training Rusty. A good way to relax after the ceremony.

After driving to her house, changing into her usual clothes, she headed to HallaVal. She walked inside, went to her locker, and pulled out her training attire. Switching from her crop top and skirt to a sports bra and small spandex shorts with boxing boots. Her training attire exposed her firm, toned body even more the cocktail dress. She exited the girls locker room and began walking to the bag room.

But as she passed by the office, a familiar face caught her eye. Again.

"So how much would a membership cost?" Arrow asked the staff member.

Arrow and the staff member continued the conversation of the semantics of membership as Era walked up and interrupted them.

"Era?" Arrow said. "OOOHHH so THIS is the gym you're always talking about training at!"

As Arrow said this, Era noticed his eyes glancing up and down Era's body. He had a tint of redness in his cheeks.

"Well duh." Said Era. "What are you doing here?"

"Oh, I've decided to try and get a bit more into fitness lately. You've been motivating me lately. I used to be on the swimming team in high school and I'm losing my physique. I'm trying out a bunch of different gyms to see which one I think would suit me."

The staff member chipped in. "Well sir, we do have a weight section and a small pool. Along with the striking area. We do offer a free one-day trial, so you can try the facility out before making a decision."

Arrow turned to face the staff member. "Ok, yeah let's do that. Can I go now?"

"Absolutely sir. Here are some complementary items." The staff member said as he handed Arrow a clean pair of swimming trunks and a towel."

Era gave Arrow a light shove as he grabbed the things from the staff member. "Ok, well I'm going to hit the bags for a little bit. Go do your little swimming. I'll come over later."

Arrow smiled and replied, "Ok."

Era headed over to the bag area. She wrapped her hands and laced up her gloves and did her premeditated light form work. Some light power hooks, jabs, and footwork. She tried to stay focused but had a slight distraction in the back of her mind as she worked. Despite going light, she had a heavy sweat going. Her hair damp from and little droplets fell off her nose and chin.

After an hour, she decided to end her workout and went to the pool area to meet Arrow as she said she would. He entire body had a slick shine from the sweat caused by her workout.

She unlaced her gloves and unwrapped her hands and walked towards the pool area. It wasn't a huge Olympic sized pool, but it was big enough for a swimmer to get some laps done in. Era opened the door, walked in, and saw a long, lean, chiseled body darting from one end of the pool to the other. Era stood there letting Arrow finish his laps. She could see that he was focused and lost in the moment of his chosen method of fitness.

Arrow finished his last lap around and exited the pool. As he turned he saw Era and gave a huge grin. Era took extra notice of his perfect, straight white teeth that made his immaculate smile that much cuter. As he walked up to her, Era eyed him up. From his feet, to his long expose bare legs, to his mid-section that only had a tight fitting competitive swimmers spandex, to his rock hard abs, veiny forearms, up to his drenched light brown hair, dripping with water.

"Ummm... Era. My eyes are up here?" Arrow said jokingly.

Era refocused her eyes, smiled and laughed while scratching her head.

"Well how do you like the gym??" Asked Era. She had clearly visible, red flushed cheeks. As did Arrow.

"I'm not quite sure yet. I do like the pool, but we'll see what happens."

The two continued chatting for a short period of time before deciding to go on about their business. Era waved goodbye as she walked away as Arrow walked towards the men's locker room to change over.

After changing over, Era walked to her car and sat in the driver's seat in silence. Lost in thought for a few minutes, she remembered that she had to wash a hamper of clothes that she had in her trunk.

Era took a deep breath and started her car. The air conditioning blasted hard into Era's face. The lower vents shot straight up her legs, sending a slight shiver up her toned thighs that transitioned up into her spine, and made its way to her previously blushed cheeks. Causing her entire body to shiver.

Era shook it off and took another deep breath. She put her car in gear and headed to the laundromat to finish her last activity for the day.

Era drove, passing through various street signs and cars. She noticed some advertisements on the way to the laundromat. Various online dating sites, birth control commercials playing in the screens in stores along the long streets. She also noticed some couples walking down the sidewalks. Some holding hands, some sitting cuddled up on benches, and some eating together on the outdoor tables of some restaurants.

A short while later, Era arrived at the laundromat. The sign above the front door read, "Amore Eterna Laundry". Era parked her car, got out, grabbed her hamper of dirty clothes and went inside.

She stuffed her clothes in the nearest washer and sat down on one of the chairs. She sat there, legs and arms crossed as she waited for the machine to finish. She still had a small pump from earlier, so her arms and chest were warm and contracted.

The door opened and her eyes moved up to see a familiar face for the 3rd time today.

Arrow opened the front door and his eyes met with Era as he walked inside.

"Dude. Why the fuck am I seeing you so much today??" Asked Arrow.

Era stood up gave Arrow a gentle shove and answered. "I have… no idea, to be honest." She had a lighthearted laugh as she spoke.

"Hey, By the way." Said Arrow. "I never thanked you for the book you gave me a few months ago. I've been grazing over it, and it's been giving me a nice bit of ideas for my spoken word performances. I really appreciate it." He was grinning ear to ear.

"No problem." Said Era as she brushed her hair to the back of her ear and smiled back.

Arrow stuffed his clothes in the washing machine next to Era's. The two continued their conversations on a variety of subjects. Arrow went on about his science classes, and Era told him all about her training Rusty. Arrow told Era about the weirdos that came up to Elysium and Era told Arrow about the variety of kids that would come through the primary school.

Era's clothes had finished in the dryer, but she waited for Arrow's clothes to finish as well. Afterwards, they continued talking as they folded their clothes.

After all of their clothes were folded, they both walked towards the exit. They stopped walking as they got to their vehicles and faced each other. Era stood there hugging her arms, smiling at Arrow. And Arrow in his clean pressed, fitted t shirt and jeans. With his giant, perfect smile, hands gripping the cart that held his clothes, his veins throbbing. A small breeze caused Era's jet-black spiked hair and Arrows wavey light brown hair to flow as it passed.

"Sooooo…" Era said. "It's kinda late. Would you like to come over to my apartment?"

Arrow gave a light blush. "I would love to, but I promised Hedone we would spend time with our parents tonight. Maybe another time?"

Era swallowed her spit that was about to turn into drool coming out of the corners of her mouth. "Ok. Definitely next time." She said as she smiled.

The two parted ways and Era went home. Era felt unusually exhausted and decided to undress and head straight to her bed to fall asleep. It didn't take long for her to drift off.

# Part 2

# "Teeth Marks"

Era found herself in a familiar place. The lower section of the cave where the Sage taught her the first lesson. The lower shrine that housed the mirror. Yet the sage was nowhere to be found. Strange that the Sage wouldn't be in what she thought was his dwelling place. She called out to him, but still was interested to find no one. She walked around and glanced at the far wall to see a small shimmer.

It was the mirror. That damn mirror that housed the creature that gave her the worst fight of her entire life. Where the creature that she had fought and accepted came from. She came close to it wondering if anything would happen this time. She stood in front of it, looking at her reflection.

She looked up and down. Examining her shoulder length black hair, dark green eyes. Analyzing every inch of her body and all black attire. For some reason, her reflection showed her wearing a crop top and an above knee skirt rather than her usual attire of a black t shirt and jeans.

As she continued analyzing her reflection, it suddenly started moving on its own and began turning jet black. Just like the creature she had fought. She jumped back and took a fighting stance. The creature moved erratically as if it was in pain, twitched, and started moving forward. Finally, it came out of the mirror, as it did before. Era's pulse raced.

Would the creature attack her as it did before? She thought she had accepted it and gained its power already. So why would it attack her again? The creature walked towards her. Slowly. Intently.

It suddenly stopped walking and stood still. It had the exact same shape and figure as Era. It breathed as she breathed, it moved as she moved. It had the same boney knuckles shape, and flowing spike tipped hair that Era had. It resembled her in every way. Suddenly, it began to transform again. Into something entirely different.

"What the hell is going on? Where is the Sage?!", yelled Era.

"Last time the Sage wasn't here to meet me, I went through a hellish nightmare. But going through it made me stronger, so if I gotta go through it again, bring it on!!"

The creature kept on shifting, growing a little taller and developing broad shoulders. Shifting and changing more and more. Until finally, the creature stopped shifting and opened its eyes. Staring directly into Era's eyes.

Era began to flush furiously red and unwillingly drool. It was the Bartender boy. It was Arrow. That Bartender boy with that charming smile of his, gazing directly into Eras eyes while giving that cute sideways smirk of his. A small breeze made its way into the room, causing Arrow's hair to gently wave. He took a step forward and Era's stance immediately went from a clench fisted fighting stance to hugging her own arms, pressing and squeezing her thighs together. A small breeze in the cave made it way up Era's thighs and caused her skirt to flow upward. The breeze sent chills up Era's spine and caused her entire body to gently shiver.

The bartender boy took another step forward, causing Era's inner thighs to gently rub together more. And with each step forward, Era began to blush with an even more intense shade of red.

The boy finally stopped in front of her. Looking directly into her eyes, not saying a word. He put his hands on her cheek and moved in slowly to press his lips against hers. Era melted and inhaled sharply as their lips met. She threw her arms around his neck and they both gasped as their tongues swirled around each other.

Throwing aside her flustered demeanor, Era gave into the passionate desire she had been holding onto for so long. She ripped off his shirt, exposing his exquisite abs and he gently pulled her tight-fitting crop top over her head, exposing her glistening, sweating breasts. Their lips stayed pressing tightly as Era began diggings her nails into Arrows back. He bit her lower lips in response to the pain and lowered his hand to start pulling off her skirt. Then he picked her up by her lower thighs onto the mat the Sage would rest on. She unbuckled his jeans and used her legs to lower them until they dropped completely down.

They continued grabbing each other's flesh and removing articles of clothing, slowly but steadily until they both had nothing on. Era could see red marks on his chest from digging so much. After more digging and biting, he was now directly on top of her. She wrapped her legs around his waist and started biting his neck. He let out a deep sigh, and Era released her grip on his neck. He then latched onto her collarbone with his perfect, rigid teeth and she let out a passionate, content moan of pleasure. They kept up the process, leaving teeth marks on each other in passionate union and sincere ecstasy.

The Bartender boy and Era lay there after an eternity of extravagant desire. Constant pressing of flesh, nail scratches, and teeth marks. Arrow looked into Era's eyes and gave that charming smile of his. Era, no longer flustered, now given to her desire looked directly into Arrows clenched tight face as he crescendos into an eruption. She gave a heavy sigh after feeling him finish deep inside her, gripped him tight and closed her eyes.

After smiling ear to ear she opened her eyes to see the numbers on her alarm clock while that annoying fucking sound wouldn't stop screaming until she pressed the off button. Never before had Era woken up with such a wet-sheeted, quivering disappointment.

# Chapter 11

# Part 1

Era got out of bed and hurriedly walked towards her closet to get the spare sheets she had up on the shelf inside. Usually slow to wake up, she was motivated out of self-embarrassment and the desire to clean up after herself. After pulling off her sheets and replacing them with sheets that weren't soaked, Era buried her face in her hands and took a deep breathe.

"What the actual fuck was that?" Era thought to herself. "I've never had a dream like that before."

Era would usually get in a light sweat to wake herself up and start her day right, but she was already wide awake, and the day had already started off incredibly awkward. She needed to clean up and get on with her day.

But it was a Sunday and she had nothing to do. The gym was closed, she hardly had any studying to do, and needed something to distract her.

Studying seemed like a viable option. It may not be necessary for the college courses she was in at the moment but going over some old notes could at least distract her from the way she was feeling. She also noticed she had some magazines on her stand next to the kitchen counter. Some magazines of the latest clothing, some about boxing news, and some magazines about new trends going on.

The trends magazine was closest to her, so that's the

one she picked up. Desperate to distract herself she opened it up and arbitrarily chose a section to read.

Apparently, a new trend of martial artists of all kinds travel to waterfalls and mediate under the waterfalls to teach themselves how to focus. This trend was picked up from an ancient practice of monks in an old dynasty. It was named "Takigyo" and was done to cleanse the body, mind, and spirit. Era read the full article for about 15 minutes over and over until she heard her phone ring.

Not one to typically receive any phone calls, let alone on a Sunday, Era was reluctant to pick up. She walked over and skittishly picked up the phone.

"Hello, this is Erebus.", She said.

"Era!" exclaimed a warm and familiar voice. "Sorry to bug you, sweetie. I was just wondering if you'd want to grab a cup of coffee to talk about your application."

After hearing the voice speak, Era realized that it was Miss Magist.

"Oh! Miss Magist! Ummm… sure. When are you thinking?" Era asked.

"It's still a bit early, so I was thinking in about an hour? There's a little coffee shop near the school called 'Kismet Coffee'. How does that sound, honey?"

Era agreed and Miss Magist said goodbye and ended the call.

Era knew the drive would be short, so she decided to

get in a bit of reading before she would shower and head over.

She sat down and haphazardly grabbed past notes to go over from her bookshelf of archived schoolwork. Some notes from Professor Friedrich's class about identity and self-awareness. "Become who you are!" was the main quote that Era had at the top of the paper.  Another section of her picked up notes was from one of her psychology classes with Professor Carl. It was about shadow work and working in the part of our unconscious mind that we don't want to accept as who we are. As she went over these old notes, she remembered a study session she had with Arrow and during that session he was explaining the process of crystallization that he learned from his geology classes. She placed her hand on her cheek and began thinking about him more.

After realizing she was doing the opposite of what she intended to do while going over old notes, she stood up, shook her head, and decided to get ready to meet Miss Magist.

She walked to her shower, undressed, and climbed in. The entire time she was in the shower, her thoughts raced. From everything. From her dream, to the upcoming meeting with Miss Magist about her application, to Arrow, to the Sage, to her classes and everything she has been learning. All the thoughts rushed in her head, like a constant flow of water.

A quick wash, drying, clothes, and a light application of makeup later, and Era was out the door. Excited to go over her application with Miss Magist. Now a bit more focused on the real world, rather than lost in her thoughts, she began to regain her composure and revert back to her usual demeanor.

Roughly an hour after Miss Magist had called Era, she arrived at Kismet Coffee. She went inside and saw Miss Magist sitting down at one of the tables with her legs crossed and drinking a huge Frappuccino with a mountain of whipped cream on top. She was intently reading a piece of paper that laid in front of her on the table. Era knew exactly what it was.

Era walked up, and as soon as Miss Magist saw her, she put her coffee down, and stood up to hug her.

"Hi honey bun!" Miss Magist squealed as she embraced Era. Era returned the favor and wrapped her arms around Miss Magist's soft, short, and corpulent body.

They both sat down. Before they started their conversation, a short young man came up to the table and asked Era what she would like to drink. Era ordered a black, bitter coffee with no cream to keep her mind focused.

"Ok, Era." Started Miss Magist. "So, your application to start working as a teacher looks good. But there's a few things wrong with what you put on your resume."

Era motioned her hands in a praying position up to her mouth, ready to receive the advice Miss Magist was about to give her.

"First of all, Era. You shouldn't use slang on applications. It's extremely unprofessional and would typically be rejected. Don't put 'I've worked at this same school for 3 years; ya'll should definitely pick me."

Era blushed as she gave an awkward smile and scratched the back of her head.

"Don't just put down whatever random thought comes into your head, honey. What you put down isn't wrong, but it's good to take what you mean and phrase it into a way that's appropriate and professional."

Era immediately thought of the flux of thoughts coming into her head all morning since she had woken up.

Miss Magist continued. "Also, you shouldn't put stuff like 'I fought competitively, I can teach some kids some basic physical fitness. Yes, Era it's true. But you should phrase it with something like, "I was a competitive athlete, and therefore have knowledge on physical training."

Era gave another awkward smile and nodded her head in agreement.

"You have all the credentials you need, Era. You've already been working at the school, you have experience in fitness to teach the kids physical education, and in a year, you're going to have a full-fledged degree. You just need to be a little more appropriate with your thoughts. I know you have a tendency to think a lot, but you need to form that overthinking into something beneficial. Does that make sense, honey bun?"

Era placed both of her hands on the back of her head out of embarrassment and agreed to everything Miss Magist was saying.

The two stayed talking for a couple of hours going over what Era should expect as a teacher. Most of it were things that Era had already dealt with. From spoiled kids and tantrums to abusive parents and dealing with Child Shielding Agents.

Miss Magist even went on a tangent about her recent application to become the school principal so she could make some much needed changes in the school in dealing with the CSA. She explained that her father imparting all his knowledge on leading as a commissioned officer in the military and teaching her about guns made her realize how many of the current educational systems were flawed and needed reform.

Eventually Miss Magist and Era decided to head their separate ways and get on with their day. Miss Magist words resonated with Era. After parting ways, Era headed home, and was intent on doing some more studying to make sense of her chaotic thoughts.

Era got home and began. She had begun forming the constant onslaught of thoughts into a cohesive and productive mindset. She rewrote many of her cluttered writings and made it all something that was more mentally accessible.

A few hours had passed, and the sun was beginning to go down. A relatively short day, seeing as it was winter.

Era began changing into her usual sleeping attire of an oversized shirt and panties and put away all of her notes.

Suddenly, Era's phone began to ring again. She seemed to be very popular today. Era walked over to her phone and answered.

"Hello, this is Erebus." She said.

An extremely familiar and unarguably attractive deep laugh made it way from the phone to Era's ears. Causing a light flush in her cheeks all over again.

"Why do you answer your phone like that?" Arrow asked. "It's so random yet formal. Why ya gotta be so awkward???"

Era lost the composure she had just reclaimed this morning and mentally fumbled to reclaim it again. "uh, uh, UH, I'm not sure, to be honest. It's just why-, why, I'm NOT SURE!"

Arrow laughed again and asked if she was alright.

In a split-second Era had a thousand thoughts race into her head again. Thoughts of confusion, embarrassment, her dream, his eyes, his voice, and Miss Magists words.

In the next split second, she took her thoughts, and formed them into some productive.

"Of course, I'm alright! You're the one that was following me around all day yesterday!" Era playfully replied.

Arrow sheepishly chuckled and pleaded that he wasn't following her at all. As their conversation continued, Era made her way to her bed. She laid under her blanket and turned onto her side as their conversation took a very lighthearted turn.

The two continued their conversation for a few hours. The topics ranged from Era being excited to see if her application would be accepted by the Primary school next year, to Arrow being excited about his upcoming spoken word. From Era telling him about Rusty becoming a new member of the boxing team, to Arrow finding a gym with a pool that would suit his desires to get back into shape.

As the clocks hands reached an unreasonable position, Era looked at it and sighed discontent-ly. "Hey, it's getting late. I need to wake up early tomorrow."

Arrow gave a long pause. He reciprocated with a sigh of dissatisfaction. "Yeah, I guess we should both probably knock out. I have an early class tomorrow too."

Arrow gave a small sigh. Era could hear that smile in that sigh, and she smiled as well. "We should study together again." She suggested.

"Yeah, definitely." Said Arrow. "I'll see you tomorrow."

"Deal." Said Era, grinning ear to ear.

She motioned her thumb to the hang up button.

"Goodnight, Eros." She said,

"Goodnight, Erebus." He said.

Era hung up, placed the phone down, and turned around. Already tired from the late night, she closed her eyes, and quickly fell into her little world.

# Part 2

# "Crystalize your mind"

Era found herself downstream of a river with grassy plains on both sides of the riverbanks. There were some sparkling stones deep inside the river and birds flying overhead. Some trees housed nests with several eggs placed neatly in the middle. Every so often a mockingbird or dove would swoop in and sit on the eggs to ensure the warmth necessary for them to hatch.

Era noticed the flow of the water and decided to head upstream. The water of the river was as clear as air, showing the contents of the riverbed. Even more stones and sparkling crystals, with an occasional fish swimming upstream and dark green vegetation growing alongside the edges of the riverbed.

The further up she walked, she noticed the water flowing more turbulent and less clear. From a slow, peaceful laminar flow to a chaotic rushing of water that she started feeling splashing up on her face.

She came close to a cliff and saw a violent waterfall

that was causing the river's upstream turbulence. The sound of roaring water and crashing waves filled the air. A fresh smell of freshwater that reminded her of the cave the Sage dwelt in hit her nostrils. Era took it all in.

An unfocused yet familiar blotch was at the bottom of the waterfall. As Era walked closer, the blotch became clearer.

It was the Sage. Sitting cross legged, with his arms in a praying position, with his head upright, eyes closed, facing directly and intently forward. As Era got closer, the roar of the crashing water filled her ears more and more to the point of not being able to hear anything else. She walked towards the side, where the waterfall was crashing down, and went up against the wall of the cliff. The Sage was a few feet away from the wall, where the water was hitting him directly on his head.

As she tried walking even closer to approach the Sage, the waterfall began slowing down. The crashing, turbulent water, eventually became a heavy laminar stream, which became a light stream hitting the Sage directly on the top of his head. Finally, no water was flowing at all.

Era saw the Sage open his eyes through the small holes that were on the mask of where his eyes were, and he slowly and intently stood up. He turned his head and then turned his entire body to face Era and walk toward her.

His mask still had leftover water on it and his hoodie was soaked to the point of it dangling lightly off of his body.

"Hello, Era." The Sage predictably said while spreading his arms and lowering his head, giving a sarcastic bow. "Fancy meeting you here."

"Don't be a smartass." Laughed Era. She was wondering what wisdom the Sage would have for her today. She glanced around and noticed some statues that resembled some familiar faces and places from her daily life. Some statues took the shape of a young boxer, a short full hipped teacher, and a handsome young man.

"Everything we have been doing has led us here, Era." Said the Sage. Era could feel an excited grin on his face underneath that damn mask.

"What do you mean?" Asked Era.

"You've been learning a lot and picking up on a lot of things I've been showing you, have you not?"

"Yeaaah?" Said Era.

"You have fought and accepted your shadow. You've learned to embrace your anger and sadness. You've even learned to accept what has happened to you."

Era looked down and started biting her fingernails. Her left arm hugged her right arm as she tried to process what the Sage was saying.

"By the way." Said the Sage. "You made a mess on my shrine."

Era began to immediately blush an intense shade of red.

She took a deep, sharp breath and clenched her fists at her side.

"IT WASN'T MY FAULT. HE CAME OUT OF NOWHERE!!" Her entire body was shaking out of embarrassment and her jaw was clenched after she finished talking.

The Sage held his fist up to the mouth portion of his mask and started chuckling lightly. Era saw him laughing and started flushing an even deeper red.

"WHY ARE YOU LAUGHING?!" Era screamed. Her fists continued shaking as they remained at her side. Her thighs were gently pressed together, and the Sage's laughter slowly came to a stop and he cleared his throat and took a deep breath.

"I have a better question." Said the Sage. "Why are you so embarrassed about it?"

Era stopped shaking her fists, but her flushed cheeks remained red. She calmed herself and prepared to listen to the next thing the Sage would say.

"You've been accepting your darkness. Your anger, your sadness, your past. You see that it's just a part of who you are. But what makes you think your urges are any different?"

Era's flushed face took a lighter tone. She uncleaned her jaw, loosened her fists, and relaxed her entire body.

"You're human, Era." Said the Sage. "Humans go

through trauma, you feel anger, you feel sadness. And you also feel attraction and urges. Why is it so difficult for you to accept that as well?"

Era took a relaxed stance, took in a deep breathe, unpressed her thighs and exhaled heavily. Her cheeks were still flushed with a light red.

"You saw me sitting under the waterfall." Said the Sage. "What do you think I was doing?"

Era shrugged, raised her hands and shoulders, and gave a 'how-the-fuck-should-I-know' gesture.

"I was meditating. Accepting and embracing the constant flow of water crashing down onto my head and letting the process form crystals in the stones all along the river you see. Do you understand how much effort it takes to let the water flow on top of you and be silently still as it flows?"

Era turned her head and looked again at the river. A beautiful scenic image, full of clear waters, gorgeous green grass, bright blue skies, and full of sparking crystals along the banks.

"If you can accept all aspects of yourself, hone it, and let the thoughts flow something beautiful can form inside yourself, and in your life." Said the Sage. "The chaotic flow can become something beautiful if you let it take form."

Era took another deep breath and heeded the words of the Sage. She looked up at him and waited him to speak again.

"Now, Era." He said as he took a step back and motioned his right hand to point where he was sitting. "You try."

Era motioned herself to the same spot the Sage was in when she had walked up to him. She sat down, crossed her legs, and placed her hands in the same praying position as the Sage. As she closed her eyes, she felt the waterfall start to flow on top of her head.

At first, the water was a small stream, equivalent of a faucet, flowing onto her head. After a short period of time, the water began to flow even heavier, and Era felt the weight of all of it pounding onto her head. She tried to maintain her composure and keep her mind clear, not reacting to the constant flow rushing onto her head.

As time went on, the water became as turbulent and chaotic as it was when Era saw the Sage sitting where she was. Now a roaring cacophony of smashing liquid, the waterfall was mercilessly and relentlessly pounding the top of her head.

But Era paid it no mind. She sat there, perfectly calm and collected. Not wincing, not whining, but accepting of the flow of thoughts that came crashing down onto her head.

As Era sat there, the water that flowed off of her made contact with the stones on the riverbed and riverbanks. Beautiful crystals formed at a rapid rate along all points of the river. The stones right below where she was sitting crystalized and began shining brightly, the riverbank began to glisten with reflected sunlight of all different colors as crystals rose up out of the stones. And Era sat there, perfectly still, accepting the crashing waters the flowed and created this beautiful scene.

# Chapter 12

## Part 1

Era was nearing the end of her college days. Coming close to a possible new career and maybe even a new life as a professional competitor. She lost the bulk of her anxiety and was filled with positive excitement.

The days she went to train, she noticed that although Rusty was doing better, he was still struggling with home life and hormones.

Era would lecture him constantly. About how he should take advantage of his anger and use his sorrow when he draws during his free time. During many of the lectures, Era would place her hand on Rusty's shoulder. He would look down and nod as she would lecture him.

Rusty's training was going well, and coach Cassius was on his way to being promoted to manager. His nearing responsibilities worried Era. He might not be able to give the team the attention they needed. A couple of ideas would sometimes cross her mind. Coach Erebus was one of them.

After finishing the training for the day, Era gave Rusty his boxing homework of the day, which mostly consisted of some morning exercises and thought experiments to help him deal with his emotions. Afterwards, She changed over, got into her car, and headed over to Elysium for some social interaction with her favorite college student. He was working tonight, and Era wanted to see him. The

conversations they had while he was working was sacred to
her.

After a short, excited drive there, she walked in the front
door and saw that the bar was close to dead. She smirked at
the thought of Arrow not needing to pay heed to customers
and focus on her as they talked.

She walked up to the main counter, and playfully
demanded a drink from Arrow. The two started talking,
even more intimately as before. No more awkward
interactions, but heartfelt words and smiles between the
two of them.

A small group of friends that Era became acquainted
with years ago waved at her from across the room. Era
waved back.

Their conversations would sometimes be interrupted by
Pepe.

"Do yur fukin job, ya idiot." Pepe would say. It's
usually all he ever needed to say. But Pepe also knew about
the two. He didn't tend to interrupt very much.

"Hey, by the way." Arrow said. "I got you something
for your birthday tomorrow. I know it's only June 2nd, but
I'm working tomorrow and wanted to give you your
present."

Arrow pulled it from under the counter and handed Era
a large, flat, and wide package. Era smiled and slowly tore
it open. It was a canvas with the taijitu painted on it.

"I know you have a lot of posters in your apartment." Said Arrow while giving a huge smile. "I figured you'd like this."

Era gave a huge grin, looked up and said, "I love it. I'm going to hang this right above my bed."

The two continued talking until Era began to get tired enough to head home. She barely drank at all. She got off her stool and gave Arrow a tight hug. Arrow returned the favor. Era caught a small scent of his cologne in her nose, and Arrow caught a small scent of her perfume from the top of her head. Arrow was wearing a plain white t shirt that perfectly complimented Era's black one. The two colors danced under the bar lights.

"Aight Arrow, ya fukin lazy fuk. Finish cleanin' those fukin glasses." Pepe ordered.

Era walked away with her gift in hand and headed to her car. The conversations and interactions were feeling so natural now. And every day she became more confident and less awkward in general. She felt like she was becoming something different. A woman so much more confident and powerful. An unfamiliar feeling to her.

She drove home and parked her car. She got out with her framed canvas and went inside. Holding true to her word, she grabbed some nails and a hammer, and hung the canvas with the taijitu over the head of her bed.

Era got ready to sleep as she usually did. Not long after changing over, her head hit the pillow and she drifted off.

# **Part 2**

# **"Duality"**

Era had been walking up a familiar trail for what seemed to be a few hours. Upwards on a trail that she had been through before. As she walked up, she came in front of a cave. A cave that was the entrance to a shrine that housed a dear friend.

She walked up to the entrance. She stood upright, closed her eyes, and took a deep breath. She felt a light breeze hit her brown skin as she breathed in. And as she exhaled, another breeze ran through her jet-black hair, causing it to loosely wave down her lower back. Her hair had grown these past few years.

Era opened her eyes and began her walk inside the trail to the shrine. As she walked, she kept her hands on the rock walls to guide her down due to the lack of light. As she had done the first time she came here.

But rather than being excited to meet someone she had never met before; she was excited to meet a very familiar friend. The same familiar aroma of fresh water filled the air. Era took in a deep breathe every so often to breathe in the sweet smell that she had missed.

She eventually came to the shrine and saw the Sage sitting on his mat. A mat that was on top of a flat rock, perfectly shaped for him to sit on. He had one leg dangling down with one knee up and a hand resting on that knee. That damn mask of his covering his face, and damn jet-black hoodie and gloves covering every inch of his body.

Era continued walking closer and closer. As she walked closer, she looked around the shrine. The same scrolls with the unlit candles below them filled the walls of the shrine. Each scroll with a barely visible but beautiful sketch of a different landscape. But there was a new scroll. One right above where the Sage sat. A scroll with a taijitu symbol on it.

She came a few feet away from the Sage. The Sage gave an unseen sad look. His mask was directed towards the ground, and he had slouched shoulders. Era had never seen his shoulders posed like that. She could feel his expressions behind his smiling, angry mask. They both remained motionless, staring at each other. Neither wanting to make the first remark nor start a conversation.

"Era." He sternly stated.

She looked at him intently, wondering what he would say next. He stayed silent for a short period of time until Era decided to just sit down on the floor. She crossed her legs and looked upwards to the Sage. The mat covered stone the Sage sat on was looked to be three feet tall. With Era being 5 feet away from him, her head had a small incline as she looked at him, while the mask covered face of the Sage had a slight decline while he looked down to her.

"Do you remember what happened when we first met?"

Asked the Sage. "You didn't even know who I was, yet you came here asking for answers. You even called me master."

The Sage had a light chuckle in his tone as he spoke.

"Era…" He said again.

"Do you remember what happened when we first met?"

Era saw that the Sage had a slight hesitation as he spoke. He had always been so calmly powerful and stern before, yet for some reason he was giving off the demeanor of a scared child, about to be ripped away from his parents.

"I do remember." Said Era. "That whole thing was insane. You led me down to the lower room." Era pointed downwards to the entrance of the room that housed the mirror.

"I fought my own shadow. I've never felt something so intense. Not even the hell house, my childhood, being bullied by the other kids. All of that paled in comparison to fighting that thing."

"Well." Said the Sage. "All of that is exactly what you were fighting."

Era cocked her head back and raised her eyebrow.

"What do you mean?" She asked.

"I told you way back then. That love and hatred are not opposites. They are sisters. They are two sides of the same coin. They complement each other."

"In the same way that female and male need each other. A man learning from and controlling his feminism side can become a stronger man. A woman learning from and controlling her masculine side can become a greater woman."

Era crossed her legs and lifted her hands in front of her face in a praying position.

"In the same way that war makes peace the treasure that it is. The darkness makes the light shine all the brighter."

Era was totally homed in on his words.

Hot and cold are opposites that make each other more relevant. Black and white. Yes and no. Up and down. Nothing and everything. Life and death. Happiness and sadness. Order and chaos. They are all different parts of the same whole."

"Same goes for love and hate. They complement each other. Do you remember me telling you that when we first met?"

Era took a deep breath, clapped her hands in front of her face and sighed. "Yes. But I still don't really understand. I feel like I felt what you meant back then, but I still don't understand it. How are they the same?

The sage put his hands on his knees and leaned forward a bit. "They aren't the same. But they come from the same emotion and passion that dwell within certain people."

"Same passion?!" Exclaimed Era. Suddenly all the

memories came back of her foster parents throwing bottles and pulling knives on each other. Child shielding agents taking Era away and bringing her back as soon as they were sober, and they would go right back to the same acts.

"That doesn't make any sense! I was a kid! That hatred was all I knew! Because it's all they taught me! It's their fault!!"

"Or do you THINK that's all you know?" The Sage replied.

"That's what I believe! It's what I've learned!" Era screamed.

"Or is that just what you WANT to believe?" Answered the Sage.

"But I need this! Everything you've been showing me us what I need!" Era yelled.

"Or is that just what you THINK you need?" Replied the Sage.

"But I've been forced into this!" Screeched Era. "It's not my fault I went through all of this! This entire fucking thing is what I've been forced to go through because of YOU!!"

"Or have you CHOSEN to do this?" The Sage said.

Era clenched her fists, stood up, and took a stance ready to strike the Sage right in that smug, smirking, angry, damn mask of his.

"Era, do you remember meeting Optimism and pessimism?" The Sage interrupted before Era could strike.

Era immediately thought of those two beings wearing the Talia and Melpomene masks, covered in cloaks that covered their entire bodies while standing on a cliff that overlooked that terrifying abyss.

"Yes" She said as she lowered her fist. "They were so weird."

The Sage raised his voice and said, "How is it after all this time you aren't getting this whole thing?" Said the Sage. "You've been learning your darkness and your light. The difference between pessimism and optimism. Other people's perspective as opposed to your own. All to crystalize your mind?"

Era had never heard the Sage speak so forcefully. She felt the urge to sit back down so he could finish his undoubtedly important thoughts.

"You're still not getting that they didn't teach you this hatred? They brought it out of you because of how sensitive and passionate you are. They weren't hateful, they were just stupid. You on the other hand, ARE hateful. Because you are passionate and very sensitive. It's for these same reasons you're teaching Rusty so well, why you're so hopelessly infatuated with that Bartender boy, why you love those kids so much. You learned hatred from them because all the passion took the form of hatred. And now it's turning into love with other people.

Era leaned her head back and took it all in.

"You know, Era. Overcoming your weaknesses and learning self-control and discipline can cause yourself to become something entirely different. Learning that passion on both ends can be very enlightening. Because if you know how bad the horrible feels, you know how good the great can feel."

The Sage took a slight pause and continued. "Take special note of your weakness. Once you master it, it will become your greatest strength. Causing you to become something entirely different. And the new person you become may drive some people away, attract others, and even make you see things entirely different. It may even make you lose sight of who you are."

# **Part 3**

*Era blinked and suddenly found herself and the Sage surrounded by a total blackness. Standing on what seemed to be nothing. Nothing was visible but themselves. Era was still sitting down, looking up at the Sage, who was now standing on the all-encompassing blackness.*

*Era looked at the Sage.*

*"Can I tell you something, Era?" Asked the Sage.*

*"Of course." She replied.*

*"This entire time, I've been suffering there with you. Feeling everything that you feel. Learning what you learn.*

*And even hurting the way you've been hurting. All this time."*

*The Sage walked a few steps until he was standing in front of her. He reached out his hand and helped her up.*

*"No matter how much you may hate what happens, what others do, or what others think. No matter how much you may even hate yourself. Just know that life is worth living."*

*The Sage reached his arms out and hugged Era. She hugged him back and heard a slight choking in his voice. She looked forward and saw a small wet spot on his chest. Her eyes shifted up and she saw a small tear coming out from under his mask.*

# Chapter 13 (Final)

# Part 1

Each new day seemed to get brighter and brighter as Era went about her life. But with every increase of psychological brightness, Era's spirit became more uneasy.

Era had been meeting up with Arrow on a nearly daily basis. The had been spending more and more time together, even going together to Arrows spoken word performances. The crowed usually gave a plethora of snaps, showing their love. Era usually showed hers with a light kiss.

She had an image of Arrow asking her out to another spoken word followed by a dinner date. She lightly blushed and gave a huge grin at the thought. Proud that she was finally ready and willing to take that step into openness, no longer remain encased in her shell. Wondering where the date would go and what would happen, she decided she would accept whatever took place.

The thought of graduating with her degree didn't faze her too much. She had learned to not let her fear of the future overtake her. However, she would hold on to the experiences for the rest of her life. She was ready to take on her new life as a teacher at Svarga primary school and a new coach alongside Cassius. She could now harness the ferocity of her anger without being consumed by it while teaching Rusty to do the same. The focus and drive of hatred without letting it corrupt her and showing him to do the same.

Things were going well. She had grown and knew she would continue to do so. Her disdain for life diminished, and as she learned to utilize her negative emotions more efficiently, she felt the majority of her anger and hatred fade away. But while this may have seemed like a good thing, something had been lingering in the corners of Era's mind.

"I don't know who I am anymore." Answered Era.

"What?" Answered Arrow while raising his eyebrow. "I asked if you wanted to go to another spoken word this weekend?"

Era awkwardly returned to reality. "OH MY GOSH I'M SORRY I SPACED OUT!"

Arrow laughed. "I noticed. You've been doing that a lot lately. Got something on your mind?" He looked at her, expecting her to spill her guts. Era did no such thing.

"Just feeling a little off." Said Era. "But yes, I would love to go out again. And a few more times after that." The date went well, and Era was set on making plans but couldn't help but feel distracted from her thought. With things looking so good, and all her darkness fading away, who was she? And where has the Sage been for the past year?

She and the Bartender boy decided to go for a walk at the park and continued walking until the sun came down. Talking about various subjects. From psychology, to chemistry, to philosophy, to the great men that built these subjects and shouldered all of new-age thoughts because of their minds.

Era headed to HallaVal to do some coaching with Rusty. During their training sessions, Coach Cassius usually let them be. Era had developed her own calm style and method in dealing with Rusty. She no longer lost her temper, and taught Rusty to harness his anger during his training. Rusty was taller than Era, now. And during their last sparring session, Era was unable to keep up and had to take a knee. Rusty respectfully helped her up and the two laughed it off. His skill was beginning to outshine Era's. More defined, muscular, with far more endurance, speed, and strength. He was ready to have his first semi pro bout as a teenager.

Still grateful for Miss Era's teachings, Rusty would constantly ask her for advice. It sounded odd hearing that deep voice of his call her 'Miss Era'. But it was a sign of an abundance of respect and admiration for his teacher. She would gently place her hand on his shoulder as she gently rebuked him whenever he made any type of mistake. Rusty paid heed to every word she said.

Despite enjoying her days and general life, Era couldn't help but feel like she was incomplete. She had been hoping the Sage would teach her something about why she's feeling like this, but he hadn't been showing up. Even when she had her hell house nightmare, he showed up the next night, fully prepared to explain what she needed. Same with her amorous dream about the Bartender boy.

She got ready for sleep as usual. Some healthy food to supplement her physical demands, a shower to soothe her body and mind, some meditation to help her gather her thoughts, and a glass of wine to feed the spirit. She hoped the ceremonies of discipline that she has been conducting was enough to summon the Sage. One last breath of hope as she closed her eyes and drifted away.

## Part 2

## "My shadow has left my side"

Era had been waiting in her lucid dreams for what felt like decades, but the Sage was nowhere to be found. Not a sneaky hand on her shoulder, a witty remark, a calm chastising, nor a cryptic quote that she would later understand. He eluded her, and it broke her heart. Every dream felt like an eternity of passive yearning. It was as if she didn't know anything without him. Not even who she is.

Being fed up and no longer content with waiting for the Sage to come to her, she decided to start searching. She decided to start with her crossroads of thoughts. She looked at the complicated signs as she walked down the road, once again walking in a full circle. But without the Sage there to hold her hand or explain what was going on. She noticed the higher man on the sign was no longer on the path. It seemed that it had been scratched out. Or maybe he also, had left.

Then the bloody road of religion, then the broken road of science. She looked in the potholes, but he wasn't there. She didn't expect to find him on the path of religion but was determined to find him. She was right to expect as such. Era continued walking each road multiple times until coming to the crossroad again. She glanced in each direction, looking down the many roads one by one. Only finding the emptiness of being without him.

She moved on and saw the lab buildings in the distance and decided to look there next. She went to the operating room where they conducted her atomic dismantling. Looking at the operating table where the Sage had clumsily opened her head and analyzed her brain by slicing it up. Still blood drippings from where the Sage cut out her heart and showed her what her genetic predispositions were and are.

The nightmare house she suffered her suicides in was no longer covered in black, nor alive and beastly. She walked inside and explored, but with no blood stains, nor broken cupboards. There were 3 rooms, rather than the infinite rooms that would trap and insult her. A perfectly normal house.

Era continued to look at and saw the patches of different flowers off in the distance. She decided to head that direction. There seemed to be more sunlight than before. She looked at the Roses. She recalled the Sage explaining that some need the utmost care but would in return become beautiful. She passed into the desert and was quickly dwarfed by all the cacti that were there. The Sage's words echoing in her ear.

"Some need the harshest of conditions to grow strong but can still be beautiful in their own right." Era looked at the flower on one of the cacti. A bright, gorgeous flower blooming on the top of the powerful cactus.

Era passed into the field of dandelions. They can grow anywhere and thrive as long as they have the freedom that the wind permits them. Era continued to look, expecting to find the moonflowers. But as hard as she tried to look, she could find none.

Era went on and on and on. Reliving the various landscapes that the Sage had taken her during her dreams, hoping more and more to find the Sage. And after going through every environment that she could remember; she came back to where it all started. The shrine.

She walked around, touching everything in sight. The scrolls, the candles, and the mat where the Sage would sit. She placed her feminine, hard knuckled hands on the mat and sighed with a tone of yearning. Wondering where he has been. Hoping he would come back. She then thought of one last place to look, she quickly turned around and walked down to the lowest room. After reaching it, she walked to the end of the room, facing the mirror.

Maybe the shadow creature would provide some sort of clue? She rushed to it and looked into it, as she had done before. She stared intently into her reflection, waiting. Her reflection gazed back at her, mimicking her every move and breath.

Finally, the image of her reflection started turning black. The shadow creature, her shadow self, had started to emerge! Era backed up in excitement, waiting for something to happen. Her shadow-self stepped out from the mirror and took a step forward. Era paused, waiting for the creature to do something as it has always done. And after looking directly at Era, the shadow creature turned its back and began walking away, leaving Era standing by herself. With every step the creature took, its footsteps became lighter and lighter, slowly fading away into nothing. And with her own shadow abandoning her, Era realized that the Sage was gone.

# Epilogue

## "The Sage of Darkness"

Era was finding her dreams monotonous as of late. No new lessons to be learned, no extravagant imagery anymore, no longer an intricate explanation of her existence. Fantasies and beautiful concepts no longer existed in her mind. Just a vivid retelling of the days as she slept. She would sometimes relive her old classes and time with friends. Sometimes reengaging in old memories. A date with the Bartender boy, a new person met at work. New kids coming into the school, kids moving out. A new training session with Cassius and Rusty, some new interns from Jannah University to work with her.

**Era had her first teaching class, full of eager young children. Some were passive, treating the class as a burden to be endured. Some excited to be around other children. Some had a tendency to throw tantrums at the slightest inconvenience. Others focused on the words and lessons that Miss Era would put before them. Era tried to teach them all in ways that would suit them. A kind word, a neat little analogy, a stern scolding, and sometimes a word with their parents.**

Eventually growing bored of her constant reliving of her days, she decided she would once again visit all the places she had visited with the Sage in the past, but without the expectation of seeing him. She knew he was gone.

Once again, visiting all the paths of the infinite thoughts. The bloody paths of religion, the unfinished path of science, and the complicated path of philosophy. After passing the crossroads several times, she noticed the higher man on the sign was no longer scratched out.

**Era and Arrow had been going to spoken words together. But rather than going together as dear friends, they would be going in hand in hand as a couple that others would strive to emulate. Arrow would give his spoken word performances, often dedicated to the strong beauty that Era resonated on a daily basis. Era swooned at the heartfelt and elegant words that her new lover would speak of her. Afterwards, they would typically head home together and enjoy each other's bodies for hours until neither could walk without limping. Some days they would talk about Arrow's job offer to work as a researcher in another prefecture and what that would mean for their relationship. It was a conversation that Era dreaded, and Arrow would constantly put off.**

**"I guess whatever happens, happens." Arrow finally said.**

**Era hugged him tightly.**

She continued on one of the roads that led to the fields

of flowers, she would look closely at all of the flower patches. The roses were the most beautiful they've ever been. The cacti were towering over her to staggering heights. The dandelions constantly blowing in the wind, being free to land wherever they could. She couldn't help but smile at how much the flower fields had grown. The roses of beauty, the strength of the cacti, and the vast freedom of the dandelions.

She looked down and noticed something unexpected and familiar. An un-blossomed dark blue flower, reluctant to open in the sun. She walked towards it and as her shadow covered it, it suddenly danced open. The moonflowers were back. However, Era paid it no heed.

She walked on and on until she reached the entrance to the shrine again. She placed her hands on the walls and walked the long cave ways. Slowly and without purpose, she breathed with every step she took. Knowing she wouldn't see anything inside the shrine ever again, she finally walked into the sacred place where her great journey began.

**Miss Magist would often call in Era to her office at the entrance of the school. The two would speak about various issues around the school and how the students would react towards taking away or adding certain rules. Miss Magist was now acting Principal of the school and had been implementing policies that would more effectively protect the children. The second a teacher would notice signs of abuse of endangerment of wellbeing of the kids, child shielding agents would be**

**notified. Most cases were worked out in a timely manner, but others were less than easily concluded.**

**Miss Magist and Miss Era would sometimes go out for lunch together and talk about their personal lives. Era was going to be moving into her new house soon and had just finished taking down all her posters and was about done packing up her studio apartment. Miss Magist was thinking about getting a temporary replacement for her so she could work on opening up an adoption organization. One that could pair up kids with responsible parents.**

**Era would tell her about her protégé that used to be in Miss Magist class, as well. Era may not have been competing anymore, but she had to get in even better shape to keep up with his progress.**

She walked towards the mirror not knowing what to expect. Her shadow had abandoned her, and the Sage was gone forever. The mirror would be nothing more than a reflection of herself. What was the point of the mirror, or even the shrine anymore? She felt a quick surge of powerful calm anger as she walked closer to the mirror. A soothing hatred, granting her focus that she would use to destroy the mirror. Closer and closer, breathing as intensely as how calm she was.

**Rusty had been training at HallaVal until getting authorization from coach Cassius and the boxing prefecture committee to get his first pro boxing match. Now roughly 18, he was about to make his debut into a pro fighter and a new life. Era had decided to stop**

**pursuing her own matches and help coach Rusty for his. Cassius supported this decision. The crowd was roaring as Rusty "The nail" walked his way into the ring. Coach Cassius, Era, and Chikara were in his corner, eager for his debut.**

**Right before they had made their way into the stadium, Rusty hugged and thanked Era for everything she had done for him. From teaching him as a young lad, to providing him with guidance, to introducing him to HallaVal, to training him every week, teaching him to control his emotions for his own empowerment. He kissed Chikara on the cheek and she hugged him tightly. Rusty no longer let his emotions control him, but perfectly controlled his anger. Powerful hooks, and overhand combos. Elusive head movement and impeccable defense. Era let out a single tear as she saw the referee raise 'The Nails' hand to signify his win.**

As her reflection came into focus, she saw the most unexpected thing in the mirror. The Sage. The Sage was standing in place of her reflection. She stood still, unreactive. As did the Sage. She lifted her arm, and the Sage imitated. She took a fighting stance as she did with her shadow and the Sage immediately became ready to fight. She swung her fist with a perfect form cross, as did the Sage, with an intent to break the mirror. As her fist made contact with the mirror, the Sage caught her fist. Era stopped and looked directly into her reflection. She slowly withdrew her fist and stood straight, wondering what was going on. Her reflection slowly turned its head and nodded in the direction of the mat where the Sage used to sit. Era looked and saw something.

Looking back to the mirror, she saw that her reflection disappeared, and the mirror shattered and was no more. Era then walked towards the mat to see what object was there, leaving the shattered remnants of the mirror behind her. As she got closer, the object became more and more familiar. She stepped up to the mat and looked down. A memento from the Sage. The mask that he wore.

Era took hold of the Mask. Gently holding it in the palm of her hands and stroking it with her thumbs. Admiring the simplistic beauty of it. The back end seemed to perfectly fit the shape of her face. It felt like she was made to wear it. She turned it around, and slowly raised it up, putting it on her face. As she did, the candles all lit and shined a beautiful light to reflect scrolls of paintings of all the landscapes she had been to in her dreams.

A scroll showing the fields of flowers and different gardens, the hell storms, the abyss where pessimism and optimism looked into, the operating room, the crossroads where all of thought would meet, the house she grew up in, the cosmos that formed her, An operating room meant to pick apart and analyze all that Era is, The eyes of strangers showing her different perspectives, lands devastated by different Hell storms, a complex web of different thoughts that all came from a common nexus, a hellhouse turned into am accepted past, a pair of opposite beings looking into an abyss, a shrine of lovers, a vast cosmos where she had been born and born again and again, a waterfall that filled a river full of crystals, and a picture of shrine that housed the Sage.

She stepped up to the mat, turned around, and slowly sat down in the same position that the Sage was in when they met. The shrine had become hers.

# ***THE END***

# **<u>Original Poetry/prose that the chapters are based off of</u>**

## **Chapter 1**

<u>Atomic dismantling</u>

Let's find out what makes you tick
We'll take you apart piece by piece

First let's dig into your memories
Repressed memories
Happy memories
Sad memories

Then let's take a look at your thoughts and emotions
The kind of thoughts you have when no one is looking
What do you think about when it's late at night and you can't sleep?
What do you feel when you're by yourself?
When kind of emotions do you have with your friends?
What do you feel when you think about yourself?

Let's begin looking at your weaknesses, strengths and interests
The things that bring you down
The things that bring you up
Things that you do to keep yourself occupied
Objects or ideas that make you smile

Now let's look at your chemical makeup
Your levels of dopamine
Do you lack serotonin?
What triggers your adrenaline?

Now let's look into your heart
Things that you live for
Things that keep you going
The people you love
I sincerely hope that I am somewhere in there

# Chapter 2

<u>"I have planted myself; this is how I grow."</u>

I am a rose. And my garden is this soft place. This climate of love and kindness. I live on love and kindness. Delicate fingers and just the right amount of water. Be gentle with me. I will die without love and kindness. But if you can take care of me and love me like I need to be loved, I will share with you a beauty like you've never seen. But if you try to hurt me, my thorns will make you bleed.

I am a cactus. And my garden is this desert. This desolate wasteland. I live wherever I can. I thrive no matter what. I even grow flowers though no one thinks I can. I don't need your help. Don't try to bring me down. I can defend myself.  I can do this alone. I will live. I will endure. I will never give up.

I am a dandelion. My garden is this vast field of nature. I will not live long. I will pass away quickly. But it is for the better. Scatter me across the world. And I will spread love and beauty everywhere if you let me.

I am a moonflower. And my garden is the darkness. The shadows are my home. And my beauty is in the nighttime. Don't put me in the sun. Don't try to make me live by your standards. I am fine how I am. My beauty is in the darkness.


<u>"How a flower grows"</u>

I'd liken myself to a dandelion
Freedom only through destruction
I see myself in the opening petals of a moon flower
Blossoming only in the darkness
I see the curse of a cactus Such enduring strength Yet unable for any
Intimacy

# Chapter 3

"<u>A Strangers Perspective</u>"

The way you see yourself
Is not the same way I see you

The way I see myself
Is not the way you see me

The way we see each other
Is not the same way
A sibling sees us
A friend sees us
A lover sees us
A stranger sees us

And you would be amazed
At the things you would learn
If you looked through the perspective
Of someone other than yourself

# Chapter 4

<u>"Hellstorm devastation"</u>

A raging wildfire
Burning everything in its path
Leaving nothing but ash
Like an uncontrollable hatred

Bombardment of winds and gusts of air
Tearing the very roofs of houses
Uprooting and knocking down trees
Like an unquellable anger

Raging ocean and tiding waves
Swallowing anything and everything
Pulling it to the depths of the depths
Like a never-ending sorrow

Earth shattering and shaking
Splitting the ground open
And consuming whatever stood on it
Like a deep rotting fear

Emotions will cause devastating effects
When left unchecked

## Chapter 5

**"Theory of Infinite beauty"**

I'm reading a book on string theory. (It's been a while) This book fascinates me because it tries to explain what everything is fundamentally composed of. Not matter, but vibrating strings of energy. Essentially atoms to atoms. I haven't finished so this is an incomplete thought, but several things that have stuck out to me.

One thing in particular that stuck out to me is everything is nothing but chance, and anything is possible. The laws of physics still apply (Newtons laws, etc.) And everything generally follows a certain pattern. If you combine the two ideas it could be thought of like this; if you know two elements react with each other because you're good at chemistry (I'm not) the chance of them reacting is 99.9999999999999999%. But because there is a slight chance that they will sit there as if nothing happened. But this is like a 0.0000000000000000000000001% chance.

I try to think about this in relation to parallel universes. It has been highly speculated that there are other universes. (black holes could possibly be portals to these other universes) But what if these universes were also composed of these vibrating strings? Furthermore, considering what I've read (again I am not an expert, I am sure I am missing a lot of information. I am not a physicist) the universe should not really exist. It should be failing, collapsing within itself, not stable at all. Even newtons laws, which have been the basis for pretty much all of modern physics, has been under assault. So many theories have been "disproven" (like the cosmological principle) and so many things are left unexplained. I love it.

So, I thought, well according to string theory anything is possible right? What if these other "universes" are also composed of these strings. So, it's possible that there are infinitely many parallel universes but none of them every came to actually be. But one did. Ours. It could have been trillions, quadrillions of years or even an eternity past until finally there was sufficient chance for the universe that we live in to come to be.

This is purely speculation, but we could be one in the infinitely number of universes to ever sprout into existence. And we live in one of billions of galaxies. In a teeny tiny piece of that galaxy. On a rock that is one of the smaller portions of a ordinary solar system in a section of the galaxy that is actually able to sustain life. In tiny section of time out of millions of years that life has been on this earth.

And you. In the midst of all this chaos, was sprouted out of millions of cells competing as the result of two people meeting in the billions of people to ever live on this planet. The chances of you existing is inconceivable, it doesn't make sense on a quantum or mathematical level. And yet here you are, reading this, living life and fighting the impossible odds that you have been given not only by science, but by the life you have lived.

This goes so much further than saying "You're one in a million." I'm not saying one in a billion. Or even a trillion. This is saying you are one in an infinity.

Do you think you're not important? Do you think you don't matter? I think otherwise. I think you are the result of something sprouting out of an impossible chance.

You are infinitely beautiful.

**Chapter 6**

Enlightenment lies in the nexus

Science and religion
Logic and mythology
Psychology and philosophy
Thought and intuition

Each just a small shard of the truth
That was once found in the nexus of existence

Each just a different path
That many minds choose to take

And in the crossroads of these paths
The unconscious
The higher self
The soul
All stand as one

<u>"The Nexus of truth"</u>

I believe that true enlightenment lies in the crossroads where science, mythology, philosophy, religion, psychology, physics, quantum mechanics, and every other field of study that describes the condition of humanity and existence meet. After all, every religion is just an imitation of a small shard of the broken truth. Science is simply trying to piece what is found together. And each one of us is just a small, imperfect, infinite piece of existence.

# Chapter 7

<u>"The bullet I put in my head had writing on it"</u>

The bullet I put in my head
Had writing on it
It said *Love yourself*

The rope I used to hang myself
Had a tag on it
Reading *Never give up*

The bottles from the pills I swallowed
Said *Believe in yourself*

The carvings on my wrist
That caused me to bleed to death
Spelled out *Have faith*

## Chapter 8

### "The difference between pessimism and optimism"

They both saw the world
Both saw the Truth behind the lies
Both see the strings and the puppet master

And they were both honest
The two both thought about the lack of true meaning
Both could see how meaningless and fragile
everything is
And neither could find an answer

Both saw the pain in the world
Neither saw a man worth any good
Both saw the evil lurking around every corner
Neither could see where the good was

But optimism had hope for better
While pessimism chose to laugh
Optimism thought that there could be something more
While Pessimism thought everything will end in
oblivion

We both look into the darkness
But here is the difference between you and me
When the darkness looks back at us
You flinch

# Chapter 9

## <u>"Fake tattoos and a shotgun you can't hold right"</u>

You're not a hardass
You're a far cry from it
Being mean and cussing is not a sign of strength
Razors are not to be used as a symbol of how tough a person is
Do not confuse cynicism with maturity

There is nothing psychotic about you
Nothing but a little kid with tattoos
And a shotgun that you can't hold right

You claim to be crazy
But you're just scared to care about something and work hard
Because you're scared to get hurt

# Chapter 10

"Teeth Marks"

If love bites
I bite hard
And my teeth are aching for some skin

If love bites
I still have scars from your teeth
Blood dripping from my wounds at your last nibble

If love bites
I seem to be a masochist
Because I like the way it hurts

Bite me
And I'll bite you back
Let's leave teeth marks on each other

**Chapter 11**

"Crystalize your mind"

Freedom through discipline
Enlightenment through knowledge
Wisdom through experience
Light through darkness

Happiness through acceptance of reality
Overcoming depression through anger
Learning to love through hatred
Learning happiness through sorrow

Put your mind through the extreme ends of the entire
spectrum
Put your body through the entire process of time to grow
Put your soul through the trials of heaven and hell
Through the process of crystallization
Become your whole self

# Chapter 12

## <u>Duality</u>

My friend, love and hatred are not opposites. They stem from the same type of passion and ideals that dwell in our souls. They exist in a symbiotic state. They are part of each other, different forms of the same element. Duality. The more capacity someone has to love, the more capacity they have to hate and vice versa. Knowing this should make you cautious. The greater someone's love becomes, the more in danger they are of being consumed by hatred. Knowing this should also make you more perceptive. The more hateful someone might indicate how badly their love has failed in the past and how much pain they're in from it.

### ***Choice and contradiction***

*Not everything is about sex*
I say as a hypersexual manic
*Love is nothing more than chemicals and familiarity over time*
I say as an absolute hopeless romantic
*Hard work is necessary for success*
I say as a cynical failure (I really did try)
*Everything is a joke*
I say as I take things way too seriously

*There is no such thing as fate*
I say while hoping something greater brings us together
*Sometimes you have to let go*
I say as I cling to you

I've been having a constant internal battle
between things I know (Or think I know)
And things I believe (Or think I believe)
A constant war
Between what I want
And what I need

A constant fight
Between who I choose to be
And what I have been forced to become

## Chapter 13 (Final)

<u>My shadow has abandoned me</u>

I have spent years
Building myself
Around things I believed was in my nature
Supplementing my perceived predispositions
And natural tendencies

Honing my anger for fuel
Utilizing my hatred for power
Molding my sadness into art
My fear into desire
And bitterness into ambition

But now
Even my darkness has abandoned me
My shadow has left my side
And after so many years
Of building myself
I don't know who I am anymore

## **Epilogue**

# **"Sage of Darkness"**

I can show you
How to fill the void

I'll teach you
To use your anger to fight the depression
How to use flaming rage
That will burn away the things that burden you
Fire that will burn away your tears

If you can't learn to love yourself (like me)
I'll show you how self-hate can be a catalyst to make
yourself better
The love that you withhold from yourself
Can be given to others

Sorrow can be used
Fuel to make you want to travel and do good
Because you don't want that sorrow in others
Chains of sadness can be turned into flowers of kindness

Let me turn your pain
Into wisdom (a different kind)
I'll make your painful memories
Into something that will want to make the world better

I'll help you learn
To see things as they are
And not as a delusional version of reality
To be unbiased and non-judgmental
How to see the beauty even though the world is imperfect

## ABOUT THE BOOK

This book has been the accumulation of almost a decade's worth
of poetry. The prologue "the worst enemy" is actually a short story
I wrote in my early 20s. It ended up becoming the prologue after
deciding to utilize the dream aspect to bring my poems to life in
the storyline. Took roughly a year to complete.


## ABOUT THE AUTHOR


Jose A. Sanchez. Former Marine, engineer, and aspiring writer.
Many of the primary themes of this story are things I've been
through and have had to teach myself. And many aspects of the
characters are aspects that I have. I love martial arts and fitness,
and truly believe that they are part of the path to healing. My love
of philosophy, psychology, poetry, and even drinking are all seen in
the story. 'Sage of darkness' isn't just a poem to me. It's one of my
driving life philosophies.